Praise for
'Luck and Other Truths'

In Richard Mark Glover's *Luck and Other Truths*, we encounter a wide swath of men – a teacher, a single parent, a soldier, a hunter, a drug runner, a police officer, a baker, a prostitute, a journalist – in a variety of landscapes (from New Orleans to the Caribbean, from San Francisco to Texas, to the waters of Florida and a jaunt to Baghdad). These men all live in the fringes of morality while trying to talk themselves straight, sometimes through a fog of drugs and drink. The volume is filled with characters who are articulate in their desperation, their desire, and their regrets. These narratives, wrought with poetic detail and heartbreaking authenticity, examine the line men walk between life and death, between hope and self-destruction. With hints of Denis Johnson and Brad Watson, Glover carves out moments of disconnection and emptiness in which everything changes for his characters. In this sense, the pieces suggest spiritual awakenings within the darkest of moments.

~ Dawn Trook, author of *Pink Parasol and other poems*

Richard Mark Glover spins larger-than-life tales of folks on the fringe in places where they tend to collect, with the focus on that great empty space known as Far West Texas. What might appear to outsiders as a whole bunch of harsh forbidding nothing – think Cormac McCarthy – these stories are filled with quirky characters brought to life by Glover's observant eye and quirk-spotting pen.

~ Joe Nick Patoski, award-winning author of *Willie Nelson, an Epic Life* and host of the Marfa Public Radio's *Texas Music Hour of Power*

Glover's stories come at you like a sucker-punch to the gut. Like Hemingway, he writes about beaten down men making tough choices in hardscrabble places: desolate West Texas, borderland Mexico, swampy New Orleans, dope-running Florida, and war-torn Iraq. And like Hemingway, Glover illuminates these planetary landscapes and desperate lives with startling details and crackling dialogue in lean, staccato prose. What luck that you've found this knock-out collection.

~ James Nolan, author of *You Don't Know Me* and *Higher Ground*

Richard Mark Glover's stories resemble the man himself, free, wide-ranging, erudite and willing to dangle over barrancas like an alpine mountaineer. From the misadventures of a Dade County cop going through burnout in the Spanish Main to a doubting soldier in the battlements of Iraq, "Lieutenant, you're a dumb motherfucker," these stories wrench the reader and make him think.

~ A.Z. Hayes, author of *The Last Peace Officer*

RICHARD MARK GLOVER

LUCK

AND OTHER TRUTHS

TRUTH SERUM PRESS

First published as a collection by Truth Serum Press, April 2017

ISBN: 978-1-925101-77-5

Truth Serum Press
4 Warburton Street
Magill SA 5072
Australia

Email: truthserumpress@live.com.au
Website: http://truthserumpress.net
Truth Serum Press catalogue: http://truthserumpress.net/catalogue/

Original cover image and cover design copyright © Matt Potter

Also available as an eBook:
ISBN: 978-1-925536-04-1

To Lori, my love,
whose honesty and will to power on
taught me numerous lessons in life,
some I'm still learning.
Her editing, thoughtfulness and
keen mapping of the emotional realm
gave insight to nearly every story.
Without her joie de vivre
and true connection with
the Southern Gothic,
this book would not have been possible.

"Da bonefish bump but no bite," Cheo said. He lifted his wool, shook his head and the dreads cascaded down his body like an explosion of snakes and would've reached his ankles except he was standing in three feet of water. In the mangroves. A fly rod in his hand. He grinned, knowing I didn't understand. I didn't. Who would want that much hair?

Contents

About the Author

Previously Published

Do You Think I Talk Funny?

People say his speech was the result of too much cocaine. But Benji Soto never used coke. Spacey, funny, odd even, his dark penetrating eyes and lanky disconnected legs – like a black and white Picasso, valeting up and down the highway late at night, five wrist watches, Manson blasting through buds, conjuring chapters of his manifesto that took in time warps and Tensegrity. He loved the color blue and hung shades of it throughout the mud-plastered walls of his adobe, indigo on canvas, acrylic – never pure enough, and, as it turned out, his fascination with indoles, that mystical molecular plant structure that only those willing to sacrifice mainstream mental health would administer daily, as he did, stirred his curiosity most often to the dead in the nearby desert, as if answers smote from calcified bones.

"Why did your friend die?" the lady asked.

"Worms," Benji said. He preferred short answers.

She studied him, the stranger, the Athenian Stranger, Heraclitus the man, bringing rural fact to life, the story of a cave, shadows, enlightenment. A local, she thought, is he kidding?

"Imperial will return," Benji said. "Space Time portal. Silver City, I suspect."

She laughed.

"Where you from?" Benji asked.

"L.A.," she said, pulling slightly on her earlobe. "What do you do here?"

Benji looked at the woman from L.A., the sunglasses, the big white clean teeth.

"Mortician," he said and put out his hand, "John Box."

She shook his hand slowly.

"No you're not."

"You're right, bu-bu busted," he said. "I'm a plumber. Plumb this pipe, pl-pl-plumb that pipe. Seems to never end."

"Plumbing or pipes or what?" she asked.

"Or what," he said looking at her with dark eyes. A menacing blue mole quartered his left cheek.

He sprinkled salt on his tilapia-on-a-stick then leaned against the Mud Shark food van crunching the fish between his teeth. A grackle pitched from an elm and a siren wailed from the highway.

She pulled out a deck of gum from her vest pocket. "I have a proposal," she said unfurling Cinnabar Red. "Drive me around, show me the sights."

A freight train rumbled by rattling the ground.

"What do you do, exactly?" he asked as the tail end of the train passed the Chamberlain Building.

"I'm a filmmaker," she said.

Benji said, "Castenada women, that's why you're here, right? Dude loved sculpture. Donald Judd. Marfa Lights. Of course they came here. It took LAPD wh-wh-what twenty years?"

She watched him now as he wadded up the waxy paper, and broke the fish stick into halves neatly packaging the components between his thumb and forefinger.

"The three missing women of Carlos Castenada's cult?" she asked.

"Not a cult," he said. "Sure I'll show you around. My wheels or yours?"

She shrugged.

"Let's take mine if you don't mind an old truck," he said, looking at her mouth.

"Perfect," she said.

"What's your name?" he asked.

"Kubrick, Leslie Kubrick."

"Related to Stanley?"

"My father," she said.

"Really." Benji said. "Really, wasn't he...?"

"No, you watched the wrong movie," she said. "'A Clockwork Orange' will tell you everything."

"Great movie, formative," Benji said. "I threw myself into it."

"The transport was phenomenal," she said.

He said, "Afterwards we stole some purses, torched a cat. Went to Effie's and bought some ch-ch-chocolate milk."

"'We', you mean you and your friend?"

"Right. Beginning of our work."

"Work?" she asked.

"Requiems. Conducting the souls," he said.

"Were you part of Tensegrity?"

His mouth twitched. "The new version." A quick smile flashed. "Erased our personal histories. I stabbed my father. Imperial didn't have the guts. May I tell you something? Have you ever stopped the world?"

"You stabbed your father?"

"Yes."

"Why?"

"I just told you." Benji pushed his hand through his long black hair.

She took a look at the alleged plumber.

He zipped his blue jacket, then pointed to his truck.

"Do you think I talk funny?" he asked as he slipped behind the wheel.

13

She stared into the windshield. "I should get back to the hotel."

He started the truck then leaned across, penned her with one arm against the seat then slammed her door with the other. She felt muscles and goose bumps. He ran the stop sign and raced over the hill past the turnout with the trash can.

"Where are we going?" she demanded.

Benji pulled a baggie from his pants and fingered a musty mass into his mouth. "Peyote," he mumbled, then he pointed in the distance. "The separate reality."

"What?" she asked.

"The bones are power," he said.

"You're a bit mysterious," she said.

"You think?"

"I think you're driving too fast" she said.

"Journey to Ixtlan," he said.

"Another book of fiction," she said.

"It's na-na-not fiction."

Benji squeezed the steering wheel. Teardrop tattoos swelled between his knuckles.

"Is that a wrist watch?" She nodded at the small box on the seat. "Don't you have enough already?"

"Number six," he said. "Balance."

She rubbed a finger across her eyebrow. "The bones, they're your father's?"

"A collection."

"You stabbed your mother too?"

"No," Benji said.

"Does she have a speech impediment?" she asked.

"Yes."

"Who else is in the collection?" she asked. "Your friend Imperial?"

"Yes."

"No stutter?" she asked.

"No."

"I don't stutter," she said.

"No you don't," he said.

As the truck rounded a corner, an empty meds bottle rolled across the dashboard and fell at her feet.

"Castenada wouldn't have let me in, you know – infirmaries. Outer ring maybe, but na-na-now I'm Don Juan."

She looked through the window watching the ground whirl past and then looked out over the plateau of cactus as the truck streamed into the strange new realm, the distant mountains shimmering, the sky an endless blue, the blue of another world.

"Castenada died of cancer," she said.

The truck crested a hill and began the descent into a valley.

"Are you ready to see the bones?" he asked.

"How long were you in prison?" she asked.

"It's the disappearances. That's why you're here, right?" he asked.

"How long?" she asked.

"I did seven," he looked straight ahead.

"Because you stabbed your father?" she asked.

"You're asking the wrong questions."

He turned the radio on then off.

"I'm not a bad specimen. Don't you th-th-think? Calendar model in Dallas once, watches. They loved my wrists, my hands, my long slender fingers. It's just the..."

He pointed to his mouth.

Further Than It Looks

When the principal introduced me at the teacher's meeting in the fourth week of the semester, he announced that I jogged during my lunch break.

"Not jogging," I said. "Sprints." Up and down the football field, I wanted to explain, steeling myself for the afternoon classes full of teenagers whose meds were wearing thin. Geography was of no interest to them; Mozambique, the Andes, the Tibetan Plateau might as well have been rows in a corn field. Austin was a free-thinking college town but high school education had been redesigned to be more compatible with the *Weltanschauung* of politicians from towns like Muleshoe, Perryton and Woodville. My classroom time was limited to teaching the small freshman brain about creationism and passing state tests.

Now I kicked at a swell of west Texas dirt under a cottonwood tree and discovered marbles in the earth, green, red and blue, shallow under thin mud like bubbles in a thick soup. With more footwork, rusty bailing wire, surfaced along with shotgun shells and a few sardine cans. I shoveled more with the tip of my boot and discovered the gray metal of a gyroscope. I brushed the desert from it, wound it and pulled the stiff string.

Man Camp – that's what the old trapper called the place. He was trying to sell it to me and this was the day he'd show me the corners. I had met him once before. He carried extra pounds on his big-boned frame and his laugh purled with a staccato vigor. He had a large ruddy face with a crooked nose and dark brown eyes that often stared. We'd sat around the fire that first time, he quiet initially, as if his way of life was too strange for me, the city boy. I'd heard the school board up in Marfa was looking for him and he wasn't sure yet if I could be trusted.

He said he home-schooled the boy, but there were no books lying around or anything in his disposition that might suggest a learned man who was able to prepare lesson plans on the lowlands of east Africa or the pre-historic migration of humans across the Bering Sea, something a fourteen year-old might encounter in school.

But as that night wore on we began to trade stories. He trapped coyote, bobcat and mountain lions. I trapped minds. He earned enough money to get by. I constantly wanted more. He ran his traps on the ranches of the Big Bend; I set 'em in a classroom. During the off-season he stayed and worked as a cowboy, branding cattle, mending fences, while I toured the country thinking the next little town might be it.

The gyroscope wobbled. It caught the edge of the table and flipped clattering against a metal pan. Then I saw the glitter of a marbled rock. I picked it up. The round end fit neatly in my fist as if the smooth grooves were designed for fingers and the opposite side was jagged with sharp cor- rugations. Teach it as the work of wind, water and time, I thought.

"Hungry?" I heard the trapper shout from across the field. A cottontail dangled from his son's grip.

We sat around the campfire in the afternoon sun as he knifed in the last bit of lard over the rabbit frying in the pan. A woodpecker screeched as the boy watched me squeeze the marble rock in my hand.

"That's a scraper," the boy said. "Apaches used it to scrape the inside of hides." He reached out and took the rock from me, then pulled it through the air in gouging half-loops. "Me and Dad still uses it." The boy pressed his lips and a sharp single note blasted through his teeth.

"He's got a toothache on account of that mare that kicked him last week. Whistling relieves the pain," the trapper explained.

Grease popped in the pan and the boy whistled again.

A roadrunner zipped under a barbed wire fence, crossed the dirt road and into a field of tumbleweed. The boy chased it. "Hey mister. Ever seen roadrunner tracks?"

I walked over and he showed me the claw marks in the sand. "Two claws ahead and two behind on each leg," he said blinking several times, "they run faster than other birds – member of the Cuckoo family."

I nodded then pulled a log out of the woodpile. Underneath, a black spider crabbed across its web bobbing in the silk, flashing the tattooed orange hourglass on its belly. I twisted a stick into the orange and watched the spider's caramel guts ooze.

"Why'd you do that?" the boy asked.

"Do you know what that was?" I asked.

"Female black widow. Can kill you. But they don't. Now we got bad luck."

"What do you mean?"

"Apache believe if you kill for no reason it's bad. And I'm Apache."

"His momma was full-blooded Apache," the trapper said, pulling the pan off the fire.

After we finished eating, the boy fingered marbles out of his pocket and set them in a circle in the dirt.

"Do you know how to play?" the boy asked.

"Line them up and I'll show you," I said.

"Got to be a circle, mister. Everything's connected."

The boy leaned in the wind and his jet black hair blew off his shoulders.

"We don't have time for marbles, son," the trapper said. "I want to show the man the corners."

We walked along a path bordered by creosote bush and mesquite. In the distance, salt cedars shrouded the Rio Grande in a lime canopy while the sun arced toward Cienaga Peak.

The old trapper pointed to a distant pole and said, "I could get electricity for two hundred bucks." He spat brown juice. "Myself, never saw any reason for it."

I stopped and looked at a meaty hind leg, checkered with flies, dangling from a wire, nailed to a corner post. Below it, laid the cocked steel jaws of a trap. The old trapper walked on, but the boy and I stopped. I threw a rock at the trap and sprung it.

"Why'd you do that?" the boy asked.

"Save a coyote."

"That's a trap for feral hog. We catch one once a month for meat," he said.

I looked at him then turned away. We climbed down the creek bank and a red-furred critter darted through the creosote bush.

"Coyote," I said.

"Nope, Gray Fox. They change color during the season."

I walked on.

"Hey Mister," I heard the boy yell from behind me. "How long you think it took the arroyo to change course?"

I turned. The brown of his skin and the color of his clothes blended in the auburn reach of the desert. He pointed ahead to a high bluffed bend.

"Millions of years," I said.

"Nope," he said. "Happened last summer."

I tucked my shirttail in and walked on.

We visited the corners then headed back toward Man Camp, in silence save the boy's occasional whistle. A long-billed bird flew over a pond in the distance. I wanted to beat the boy to its identification and quickly said, "Kingfisher."

The old trapper looked at me and the boy giggled.

I glared back.

"There's a desert mockingbird. That's igneous rock. Over there's Micky Mouse Nopal," I said, pointing there, there and there. My urge was to bamboozle the boy, to pull the rug out, regain teacher status, up-end the classroom as the freshmen had done me.

The boy turned and walked away. I lost him as an audience, just as I had lost the freshmen on the first mention of demographics. I wondered if blaming the meds and the state curriculum was really the problem.

In the east, a crescent moon glowed between jagged peaks and a north wind blew across my face as I sat under the cottonwood. The boy had run off to catch fish and now in the twilight he stood holding a stringer of small bass. The old trapper dropped to his knees, cracked branches and set them for a fire. The boy whistled and the trapper struck a match. High-pitched yips rolled across the valley. A howl followed, then a cacophony of coyote song filled the air. We listened, eating the fish, pan fried in oil separated from my jar of organic peanut butter.

I asked about the Apaches.

"Plenty of sign 'round here. Mostly arrowheads, but we've found a few spearheads from the earlier people." The trapper pushed his cowboy hat back and the glow of the fire reflected in his eyes.

The boy handed me a flint rock with pockmarks. "You can tell a worked rock by the percussion bubble made when it's struck," he said, then added, "We found it on top of that hill." He pointed in the darkness.

The father chuckled. "Tell him what we call that hill."

"We calls it, 'Further Than It Looks'," the boy said.

A log popped in the fire.

"What do you know about physics?" I asked as I wound the gyroscope.

It whirled on the picnic table. Then with the loss of inertia it flipped and fell into a pot of beans.

The boy whistled. "For a minute there, it had a loophole with gravity."

"That about sums up Newton," the father chuckled.

I looked at the father and noticed for the first time the pen and pencil set in his shirt pocket.

I asked the father about his plans.

"Lesson plans, teacher?" He grinned.

"No, I mean life plans."

"Life plans," he rubbed the stubble on his chin. "Maybe I'll go back and finish my degree." He paused and stared at me, then continued, "Or maybe we'll go down to Paraguay. They got some big cats down there."

"Degree? I mean Paraguay?" I squirmed.

"Yeah." He paused and looked away. "Paraguay." He pushed the heel of his cowboy boot into the dirt. Then he stood, split a log with the axe in one blow and tossed a piece of the splintered wood into the fire.

"What degree are you working on?" I finally asked.

"Biology." The father stared again and I looked away. Then he asked, "What do you believe in?"

Surprised by the question, I sat up and gave my pat answer, "I'm an agnostic Catholic."

"No, no," he chuckled. "I mean what do you think about raising boys in the wild?"

"Oh," I said.

I stood then walked toward a dead limb that lay under the cottonwood. I dragged it into the fire as I thought about his question. The boy whistled.

"If whistling relieves the pain, then maybe you're on to something," I said.

The father looked at me.

I pulled my boots from the fire's edge.

"Your fire is big," he said.

"Big, too big?" I asked.

The old trapper picked up a sketchpad from the table. Then he tore a page from the metal coil and handed it to me.

I looked for a drawing, a painting, a sketch, some words, I checked both sides, but it was blank.

He grinned, then stood up and walked away.

From the window of my camper that night I watched as they spread their bedrolls out next to the fire. I heard the father say, "Good night, son."

"Good night, Dad."

A week later I strolled through the region's natural history museum and passed by a collection of Native American artifacts, neat and labeled in a glass case. Mounted in the background was a hide scraper similar to the one at Man Camp. I asked the curator if they were still used. Her eyebrow cocked up.

"No," she said. "They don't do it that way anymore." She grinned, turned and walked away and I looked out the museum window, south, toward a place called Man Camp.

Window Cleaner

Peter pulled the squeegee across the glass anticipating a slurp but rather it screeched like a bird. He glanced the six floors below as he deftly wet the squeegee again. Pedro stood on the sidewalk, looking up, his big black mustache covering his upper lip and his arms raised and hands open, signaling "Ready?" But it wasn't Pedro. It was the new guy. Peter pulled the squeegee again from the di-water, and made the final sweep. Perfect zing, a good clean window. In Mexico City, where little is clean, a good clean window says something.

The next morning Peter stood with Natasha next to a large alabaster vase between the two sets of elevator doors inside the reception area of Clinic 236. The elevator doors on the recently completed West Wing were clean, large, and fitted with an electronic floor indicator. A brass floor indicator with Roman numerals hung over the smaller elevator of the adjacent original building.

Outside the smog hung thick and gray and smelled like a garage that had gone up in flames and simmered with just enough fuel to keep a hodge-podge of a thousand chemicals smoldering.

"Do you want a Coke?" Natasha asked. She had taken off her scarf and placed it across her arm.

"I like that look," Peter said, nodding toward a tall man who stepped into the small elevator with Roman numerals. The tall man wore a navy blue suit and gripped a wad of cigars with pink bands. He smiled as the elevator door closed.

"I'm going to have a Coke," she said.

"Maybe you shouldn't."

"Why not? Either way a Coke won't matter."

Peter straightened a bill and slid it into the machine. A light flashed. The Coke clunked on delivery. He pulled it through the hinged flap of the slot. It arrived cold and wet.

"What are you doing?" she asked.

He had lifted the Coke to his mouth.

Natasha turned and looked out where a group of women waited for the airport limousine. Slender and well-dressed they did not speak amongst themselves. Some had overnight bags slung across their shoulders.

"Here, I saved you some," Peter said, holding the Coke in his hand.

She waved him away then walked toward the West Wing elevator, the one with the electronic floor indicator.

Peter followed. "I'm sorry," he said. "Here." He held out the Coke.

"Do you think you can buy your way out? Do you think you can just buy toys and call yourself a father?" she asked.

She looked at him then at the mold growing on the window.

The blue dot hit "1" on the electronic floor indicator and the clean, large elevator doors opened. A slender lady with a chalky white face and a black overnight bag stepped out. The foxtail of her shawl hung down and bounced off her back as she walked across the tiles of the reception area.

"Do you always have to belittle me?" Natasha asked.

"I don't, in fact just the opposite." Peter grinned, looking at her abdomen, then added, "We could take a cab and have lunch at Beto's before you decide."

Natasha looked through the window again. A young woman in maternity clothes sat on the bench at the bus stop with her children.

"I'm not hungry. I wanted a Coke."

"There's some left," Peter said, shaking the can of Coke in his hand.

"I don't want anything you've touched," Natasha said.

He looked at her then stood aside. An orderly pushed a pregnant woman on a gurney into the small elevator. A white sheet covered her from neck down and a little girl in yellow pajamas followed.

Natasha glared at Peter. "Muscovite," she said.

Peter lifted the Coke. "To all those in Moscow who are not represented," Peter said. "And never will be." He brought the Coke to his lips and drank it down.

A woman with white hair, a cane, and a seeing-eye dog walked through the revolving front door of Clinic 236. She stopped and sniffed as if to smell her way.

"There are things that matter, Natasha," Peter said.

"They are not essential," Natasha said. She looked out the window. "Nothing but Russians in Mexico City, Russians and Chinese."

Natasha pushed the lit button on the new elevator.

The elevator opened. She stepped in and stood next to three female nurses.

"Floor, please?" one nurse asked.

"Floor nine," Natasha said, "Termination," her eyes fixed on Peter's as the elevator door closed between them.

Peter looked at the floor indicator and watched the blue dot glide up. Then he dropped the Coke can into the rubbish and walked through the revolving doors. The glass was clean and Peter thought about Pedro and all the revolving doors they had cleaned together. Thousands of doors and windows – tons of glass, cleaned and dirtied again, but always dirtied in a new way and then cleaned. Clean enough to matter.

Outside, Peter imagined how the sun must look above the thick skirt of smog. Tomorrow he thought, tomorrow I'll take the bus and go outside the city and find the sun.

He stepped into a curio shop on Calle Zaragosa and picked out three straw finger stretchers. He put twenty pesos on the counter.

"Kids love those," the clerk said.

Peter smiled. He wanted to hurry now and get out of the shop.

"How many kids do you have, three?" the clerk asked.

Peter looked at the clerk and blinked. Tears began to drip down his cheeks.

A couple at the magazine rack turned and looked at him.

"I'm sorry," the clerk said.

"No. It's OK," Peter said. He sniffed back the tears.

"They're for my friend Pedro's kids. And for the kids on the sixth floor and for all the kids in Russia. And all the kids everywhere. And for the kid being sucked out of Natasha right now." He looked at the clock on the wall. "Right about now, I would think."

Hillbilly Armor

After emailing my wife to tell her I wasn't dead, I walk back to the Quonset hut and lie down on my bunk. I don't even try to sleep. Diesel stinks up my fatigues and the crusty blood on my skin powders against the Dacron of the sleeping bag. I take a swig from a Coke, push play on the iPod, and light up a Marlboro. Alone in the dark, all I can think about is the smoke curling in my lungs.

Earlier in the day our Humvee had been hit. We were on reconnaissance in Sadr City, the poor-town of Baghdad. Filmore drove and I rode bitch. Jackson sucked a Kool in the back prepping bullets for the fifty-caliber turret gun and Menard squatted looking for 5-Ds on the road ahead through the red, white and black images of the thermal scope.

A 5-D is any Muslim who makes roadside bombs or IEDs as we call them. It's a five-part team: a digger, a dropper, a detonator, a deceiver, and death. The digger is usually a farmer or peasant who's paid to dig a hole in a strategic location, like a road. The dropper, sometimes a kid, drops the small bomb frame in the hole and keeps walking. The detonator man comes at night and sets the charge and covers it up. The deceiver is the guy with the big smile for all us Americans. When our vehicles get close, the deceiver loses his smile and signals death. Death makes the call that triggers the bomb.

We had left the green zone and wheeled our Humvee toward Airport Road. They say it's the most dangerous avenue in the world. Concrete barriers on both sides and scorched marks to remind you: never go uncovered on this route.

An Abrams M1A1 tank came slinking by. We all watched the hard beige lines cut through the hot air, black smoking, big steel on concrete.

"Seventy-two tons of pissed-off metal," Jackson said. Smoke streamed from his nostrils as he pushed the ammo box through the hatch.

The early model Humvee, like the one we were patrolling in, are known as cardboard coffins. Compared to an Abrams it's a skinny dick. They shipped 'em across without factory armor, and no firepower.

At the bone yard, the week before, we had stripped metal from a few choice carcasses. Filmore and Menard, both welders from Alabama, fused our doors with a mishmash of anything metal, canon bars, trailer struts, even a ten-lug wheel from a smoked tanker – hillbilly armor, we call it. They forged a bird house in the back too, for the big gun we lifted out of a dead Stryker. But we couldn't prep enough steel in time to line the belly.

Jackson's Zippo had quit. He shook it but it wouldn't flame. I don't think I can remember him without a cigarette. He poked it in my fire and rolled his black eyes up at me as he sucked in fresh nicotine.

"Sarge," he said. "Whatchu living for?"

Female vocals croon through the headphones and I get to thinking about my wife. We've got a son, 18 months old. She brought him over to her mother's a month ago and hasn't been back. Says she's taking care of her grandmother in Tallahassee, but I know her ex-boyfriend lives there too.

I take another drag of the Marlboro and blow rings into the dark. The smoke inside the Humvee was thick, black, sulfurous. The explosion lifted us up and we bounced down hard on our side and rolled. The diesel ignited and orange heat sprayed through the cockpit. Shrapnel clusters tore through the rear of the vehicle piercing Jackson's body with shards from the floorboard, the axle and wire from the Goodyears. I heard the low pitch of his last word, "God." He couldn't even finish. It was some kind of prayer. Jackson was always praying. He started 'em off with God, never Lord or Jesus or Hail Mary, just God, like he was about to cuss.

I look over at the cell phone on my locker. I could call her. Say hello to my son. Of course, they wouldn't be together.

"Who's this?" A man answers her phone.

"Gina's husband. Who the fuck is this?"

"Hello," Gina says.

"Who was that?" I ask.

She tells me it's the nurse for her grandma. Then admits it's Larry, her ex-boyfriend.

"We're just friends," she says.

"Friends? I'm killing the enemy and you're fucking your friends."

She says nothing.

"It's over," I say.

"It might be the right thing to do, Michael," she says.

Holy shit. I didn't mean it. I thought she'd reason with me. I wanted her to say, "I'm so glad you're alive. I can't wait until you get back home."

But it's done and deep down, I know it's over, it's been over. It was over the moment I waved from the tarmac in the good ole U.S.A.

Hey, I never loved her. What's love anyway – hormones? It's like war, get all juiced up and live or die. Some die sooner. Some throw up. And the Earth keeps spinning. But what a butt – goddamn, finest ass in Florida.

"Gina?"

I throw the Motorola across the room and light another Marlboro.

When I get back, if I get back, I'll rescue my son, Marlon. Raise him to be a good boy. Teach him Arabic, how to bend a note on a harmonica, and write poems about birds and the full moon. I'll raise him far away from her and my Uncle Henry, the soldier of our family, the one I wanted to be like. My dad used to pat my head but Uncle Henry brought me toy guns and army helmets. Dad would push his glasses up in the Daytona sand and lecture about seagulls but Uncle Henry would go out in the woods with me and we'd hide and shoot it up. Then I began to notice girls and cool mornings and I knew I wanted to be just like Uncle Henry, buff, uniformed, lit-up. My dad would watch me from a distance but Uncle Henry was who I wanted to be.

Lieutenant Hamlet walks into the Quonset hut. He wants me to take a shower and clean the blood and diesel off. He says, "It'll make you feel better." I tell him I feel fine and very good about everything. I like to smoke in bed in the dark and smell my day's labor. Then I tell him about my wife. Pray for her to be reasonable, he says. And I say, no I'm a soldier in Iraq, I'll pray for her to be unreasonable.

"We'll all receive a medal for today," he says.

I watch his shadow against the wall. He wasn't with us today so I'm trying to piece together the "we" business.

"Lieutenant," I say, "Can you tell me one thing?"

"Go ahead."

"Why the fuck we over here anyway?"

He looks at me with his blue eyes and spreads his arms like he's about to prophesize and says in the quiet of the hut, "Because God requires righteousness."

I joined the Army when I turned eighteen. At the time, the chance of combat was slim. Then Bush gets elected, then 9/11 and all of a sudden I'm a sergeant.

"Lieutenant," I say. "You're a dumb motherfucker."

His eyes narrow and he raises his chin and says, "Get some rest, Weinert. You've been through a lot today. I'm going to forget you said that."

Outside the glow of dawn finally melts the night. The wind blows and sand smacks across the thin hut walls. There's a noise in my head and it won't go away: qua-qua, qua-qua. Menard hobbles in on crutches. He's all banged up.

"Hey, man, what the fuck?" I say.

"What the fuck, over," he says. He leans down in his bed and drops the crutches. They bounce on the floor. "Pull the shade, will you? Sleep, man that's all I want."

I close the blinds and turn to look at him. He's already out. I walk out into the new day toward mess to get some smokes. A beige tanker pumps diesel as the sun low in the eastern sky bulges over the endless sand. My legs feel heavy and everything I think about has orange in it. Like all my thoughts are wordless blobs of melting orange. And the head noise: qua-qua, qua-qua.

The lieutenant sees me from the door of his hut and yells out at me. "Weinert, take a shower, change your fatigues and go to the medic. I want you checked out. And I need to know by 1200 Saturday if you're re-upping for another tour."

He's all pumped this morning, different, like maybe he's pissed off at me and wants to change the relationship. "Yes sir," I say, and salute the motherfucker.

Inside the medic tells me to put out the cigarette and take off my glasses. He wiggles his light into my eye and then the other. "How do you feel?" he asks.

"I feel great, doc. I'd like to kill a bunch of motherfuckers today."

He looks at me. Then says, "Are you having any visions?"

"What do you mean, visions?"

"Hallucinations, blurred eyesight, irregular coloration."

"No, sir. I want to report back to duty."

I walk across the camp and stop at the port-o-shitter. The piss level reaches halfway up the funnel. Turds float just under the rim. In the next booth over I hear some guy spanking his monkey. "Hey shut-up!" I yell, trying to concentrate over the thumping meter.

Two plastic beige doors open simultaneously. He's got three stripes and a diamond. Trumped, I keep walking and stop at the lieutenant's office.

"Lieutenant, I've been RTD'd and wish to re-organize my squad."

"Get some rest, Weinert. Two replacements come Friday."

"Friday? There's some 5-Ds out there that have fucked up my men. And killed Jackson. I can't wait that long."

"You'll do as I say, Weinert."

"Lieutenant, I need to take care of business."

"This war is not a one-man show."

I light up a Marlboro and look at him.

"What college did you go to, Lieutenant?"

His skin is pale, reddish in places, like mine.

"South Carolina State. What about it, Weinert?"

"You ever killed anybody?"

"No," he says. "I never killed anybody."

Jackson is dead. Me, Menard, Filmore, and the lieutenant live to see another day.

They issue another Humvee, the latest model with factory armor and a 7.62 turret gun. Filmore drives. Menard is back in the hospital, indefinitely. The two new guys, Paige and Gonzalez, ride with us. They've been on the ground twelve hours. We're looking for Muslims with cell phones.

Dark sweaty men in greasy white tunics groan face down on the earth floor. Their women wail in the corner of the mud house, watching. I swing my shotgun out and aim at the women. "Shut the fuck up!" I yell.

Paige asks, "Sarge, what do you want me to do with them?" He stands over the wailing women with his rifle pointed at the ground.

"Speak Arabic. Didn't they teach you to speak Arabic? Ask them to politely refrain from crying."

The two-room hut smells like piss and smoke. Candles flicker. Orange creeps.

These could be 5-Ds. The world would be a better place without them, at least my world. I swing my shotgun away from the screaming women and butt-pop the head of one of the men. I have my finger on the trigger and think: Boom boom boom. No more bombs for them.

"Sarge, I didn't learn Arabic."

"Paige," I say. "Can you sing like a seagull?"

The kid is green. I could use a good man like Jackson, right now, but he's dead, gone forever. Except that I saw him last night. His blue lips whispered out of the desert floor, "Whatcha living for, Sarge?" I wedged myself between the particles of sand and thought about his question. God's brain lit up before me as I watched the circuits dial death, and then Jackson appeared leaning against what might have been all the answers in the world with a pack of Kools rolled up in his

T-shirt sleeve. I wanted to hold him and feel his breath, his skin, his wounds.

"Do you want them dead, Paige?"

"What, sir? You mean kill them? Right here and now?"

"Yes, I mean kill them dead. Make the decision, Paige. It's your entrance exam."

"No, sir, we should take them prisoner. In accordance with the convention."

"Think again, Paige."

I strap my shotgun and pull out the Beretta. Pistols are more efficient. The mess a shotgun makes is really nasty. I wrap my finger around the trigger and slide the short barrel into the thin hairs of the first man's head.

One of the women shrieks.

Paige strikes her between the eyes with the butt of his M-16. She drops to the floor. I nod at Paige. Finally I see signs of his training.

A candle falls in the corner, and a naked baby crawls across the floor. Paige swings his weapon.

"Easy," I shout.

I pick up the boy and hold him in my arms with the pistol still clenched in my fist. He whimpers and I rub his head. He wraps his arms around my neck and squeezes. The women sob. One steps forward with her veil drooping below her dark wet cheeks and holds out her arms.

I hand her the baby.

"Let's go, Paige."

"But, Sergeant . . ."

"Move it." I turn to the Muslims in the dim lit room. "Ma' Al-Salama," I say and walk out.

I climb into the Humvee. "Come on, Paige" I yell. "Get your ass in here."

I pop a Gatorade while a dead song from Metallica leaks out of Filmore's headset as we motor slowly down the hill, the

34

knobby tires clicking against the cobblestone road, echoing against the gouged-earth buildings. It's curfew and there's no lights. Each corner is blind. Each rattle, each zing – every little microscopic pop is a new chance at death. My head hurts. I want to wrap a bandage around it, tight, and cover my head so I can't hear or see or know anything.

Back in the zone, I crawl up into my bunk and lay there. I'm out of smokes but too tired to get up. In six hours the U.S. Army wants to know if I'm up for re-up, another twelve months of war. Got my whole life ahead of me. And an ex-wife. And a son.

In the distance I hear sniper fire ping and thud against endless targets. Incoming mail rattles the walls.

"Jackson, is that you?"

Seagulls, I hear them, qua-qua. They're flying over the sand and the man with the glasses stands and waves and gets smaller and smaller.

Our Lady

The Mexican flag rippled above the parking lot then slacked as I slid out of the Ford. I walked toward the racetrack and found a spot along the rail down from the noise and metal of the grandstands then watched the Ford pass through the exit gate. I checked my watch. A thermometer on a pole with a faded blue Pegasus painted underneath registered one hundred and eleven. I rolled down my sleeves then saw the horse. She lay on the ground. Her muscles bulged. She tried to get up.

"Bad luck," said a young vaquero standing next to me.

A woman dressed in white walked toward the horse. She tipped her hat against the sun and strands of blonde unfurled and bounced across sweaty cheeks. Her rounded face gave her a moon-like look, intense atop a short and squarely built body. She stood above the lame mare now and dropped to her knees offering words. The horse's head lifted then fell back against the hot desert earth.

About eight of us stood nearby, unassociated, watching the gringa. "This horse is suffering," she announced in border Spanish. She checked the mare's pulse, felt its forehead, and offered us theory on organ damage and duty. Her mouth moved energetically but there was no movement in her eyes, only a piercing gaze. Then, perhaps to generate guilt among Catholic hearts, she mentions Via Dolorosa, the avenue of pain Jesus allegedly walked on his final day.

We stood heavy in her presence, clumsy under the blazing sun.

The gringa eyed us one by one.

"You lowlifes are allowing this animal to suffer in the worst conditions," she said, her venture down Dolorosa gone. She leaned over the mare, stroked its neck. "Bring water!" she shouted.

A few pointy boots poked the earth, eyes flickered, bodies leaned as we waited for this feminine command to melt in the air like the race dust and bring back the uncontested day.

Then one brave vaquero informed the gringa that a priest has been sent for to carry out the last rites. After that, of course, the horse would be shot.

"Shot?" she questioned. "This horse is in fine condition except the leg." A thick brow quirked under the shadow of her hat.

A man in black with the ivory grip of a pistol showing above his belt picked his teeth in the shade of the weigh station. A dust devil whirled in the field behind him, lifting trash in its suction. She eyed the man then turned. We watched her march across the white caliche of the parking lot.

A gun exploded. Racehorses galloped down the track spraying the dust of the desert into the air. The rising smut dimmed the sun. A green lizard scurried. Red vested mariachis walked by. Through the white dust I saw a caracara gliding in the sky.

I wiped my forehead, checked my watch and looked for the return of the Ford.

The gringa appeared holding a gallon jug of water. She poured it over the mare rubbing, murmuring in low pitches. Then she looked at us.

"Are you human?" she asked.

She poured more water on the horse. Heat simmered off the black hide.

A man with red-copper skin and a cowboy hat slunk toward the horse then felt along its leg. He mumbled, turned and stood back among us. The gringa smirked.

"How much does the male brain shrink in heat?" she questioned. "Totally? Or do you not have brains?"

Cheeks twitched. It felt hotter.

A pick-up with a horse trailer backed up to the mare. The driver got out, stood, lifted his hat, mopped his face then scratched his head. He walked to the shade of the grandstands.

"Help me get the horse to the doctor," the gringa commanded.

We hunkered along the backbone of the beast and pushed our hands into the wet muscular flesh. Three hooves kicked with discordant thrusts, hot lies in the Mexican air. The mare snorted. The mass was too much. Her limp leg a dead snake.

"You speak Spanish well," I said kneeling next to this lady. "Where did you learn?"

She studied me then looked back at the mare.

"I speak Spanish in the present tense," I volunteered. "Can't seem to get beyond it."

"The present is a good place to be," she said in English without looking up.

"You live here?" I asked.

She cut her eyes toward the racetrack, then looked at me. "You're a journalist, aren't you?"

A black SUV drove by, the tinted passenger window filled with a dark mustached face.

"Don't let them find out or you'll be the one shot," she said. "Do you know what this place is?" She nodded toward a low crest in the hills. "See the buzzards? They drop the bodies there."

"You know this place well," I said.

"These are my people," she said. "This was my parish."

A priest in full cleric climbed out of the back seat of the SUV. He stretched then walked toward the horse. He stopped and made the sign of the cross. Our Lady looked up.

"Hello Kathleen," the priest said. "How have you been?"

She looked away.

"I must prepare the horse for the afterlife," the priest said.

"How much are they paying you?" Our Lady asked, her eyes now in full focus with his.

"The owner of the horse is a parishioner," the priest said.

"He's a Zeta."

The priest took a long look at the former nun then kneeled at the head of the horse. We backed away and stood behind Our Lady as she sifted sand through her hand, the grains washing between her fingers, splashing against the belly of the horse.

"Last rites," she said looking again at the priest. Then she turned and walked away.

She grew smaller and smaller in the parking lot, thinning into the white caliche, waning, slipping away while the eight of us, collectively pained under the furious sun, watched as if something good had been taken from us.

Birds

Lena, Little Joe and me sit down at the booth at Jovina's Café. The smell of fried bacon floats in the air and Johnny Cash plays on the jukebox. The air conditioner rumbles, spitting out too cold air pushing the plastic drapes away from the window. My head hurts. I want to take my cowboy hat off but the empty rack at the door reminds me, nobody takes their hat off in Pulvo City anymore.

"Coffee?" the waitress asks.

Outside dark envelopes of fowl swoop across the sky in search of a refuel station. The mulberry trees, loaded with fruit, are their favorite stop. In the summer heat it's only a few days before the berries ferment and turn to nuggets of high-potency wine. The birds know this, they're all over town loaded on the purple juice, flying kamikaze, flying into walls, some just falling out of the sky.

I think the birds are trying to tell us something. Some folks think animals got nothing to say. But if you listen real close, dogs can talk and cats, they're never wrong. Birds acquiring a taste for liquor is proof of evolution. Birds know things. Last month I heard them singing, Mole, Mole. Last week I went to Mole's funeral. There's been a bunch of funerals this year. Teary-eyed folk everywhere you go. God, I hope they don't cry at my funeral. Gives me the notion not to never die. But make no doubt about it, there's bad luck in the air. We got a drought going something fierce and all this death, Mexicans and Anglos croaking like there's no tomorrow.

It was a closed-casket service. Pallbearers laid Mole's coffin in the ground as the preacher stood over the loose dirt and said after the final prayer, "Keep your hats on men. We're going to try and change our luck around here."

At the wake I asked the preacher if he listens to the birds. He blinked, swallowed his potato salad then looked me square in the eye. "Fear not about the birds, son, but the purification of your soul."

Maybe my soul does need cleansing. A good rain to wash away sin and drought. But what kind of a preacher calls for luck? They're supposed to know. If you don't know, you shouldn't preach. Birds know. If we're going to keep our hats on, we might as well give the birds their due. Course I keep my hat on too, except when I go to sleep at night. Generally, I sleep with my jeans on and my socks and depending on the temperature a T-shirt or my thick gray long sleeve. Under the overpass you need to be ready. Big night rain, take all day to dry out. When it's real cold I sleep in Mr. Garza's Ford but he's a smoker and that tends to offend me. Of course I used to sleep in a house in a bed next to Maria. Things were going good for us then Murphy Mitchell fired me.

I wanted to be his butcher. I'm right good with a knife and friendly toward your average customer. I know how to hang slabs, trim fat and package. And it would be my pleasure to save those cheeks for Mr. Gonzalez, or hooves for Mr. Smith and more than ready to trim out an extra lean cut for Ms. Sanchez. But Murphy Mitchell kept me as a bagboy.

I refused to bag one day and Jill, his high-falutin wife, dressed like she was going to opera, was rearranging the gum display acting like my revolt was inconsequential. Then she walked over to the mic and called her husband down from the booth. He came walking down the aisle with his boots smacking the floor and his bloodshot eyes darting between the cereal and paper towels and fired me there in front of Cash

Register No.2. I could smell his whiskey. I think that's when my headaches first started.

He died a few weeks later.

After I lost my job I started supplementing my condition with Sotol. It's a cactus beverage. I like to drink it with Pepsi-Cola and find it good for headaches. Maria loved it. Too much. She loved flowers too. I used to bring her the old ones they threw out at the store. She liked the yellow mums when they weren't too brown around the edges.

We'd go up the hill with our mums, drink and talk about cattle. Her daddy was a cowboy. I never much cared for cattle. Dumb, real dumb animals. We'd get to talking and she'd get all buzzed and tell me how low butchers are on the food chain. Try and tell me loin and backstrap are the same thing. Well, hell, I know my cuts. Piss me off.

She disappeared. Cops came around last week asking me questions.

Little Joe yawns and rolls his good eye over at Lena. She's fumbling for a cigarette.

"I don't think they let you smoke in here," he says to Lena.

She fingers the cigarette back into the Cowboy pack. The waitress comes with three coffees.

"What's it going to be?"

We order eggs, bacon, toast, then Lena asks me, "What happened to Maria?"

"I don't know," I say. I put my hands under the table. Sometimes they make me feel uncomfortable like they don't belong to me.

"Yes, you do," Lena says. She got that look going on like she knows something.

"Why'd she leave?" she asks, rolling an empty pack of sugar between her fingers.

"Who knows," I say.

"You were crazy in love when you met," Lena says.

"No, I wasn't."

Lena shakes her head and swirls the coffee cup in her hand. My fingers tap on the underside of the table.

"I'm thinking about going back to school," Little Joe says.

Lena looks at Little Joe then says, "First time I met Mole he's standing at the bar kinda checking me out. 'You don't know nothing about Mexicans,' he said. And I stare back at him, you know, I'd never seen him before, really and this was over at the Chaparral and I'm usually the only gringa there, but I like the place and all and well I always wanted to be a singer and my daddy said I'd be a singer some day and then he go off truck drivin' and I wouldn't see him for a long time and well anyway I started singing Cante y no Llores. I finish the verse and Mole stands up and starts clapping, smiling like and then the whole bar starts clapping and then he says he wants to marry me." She chuckles. "That was the first time I ever met him."

Myself I never really cared for Mole. He always seemed kinda uppity to me. Once he told me I didn't have the brains to be a bagboy much less a butcher. He's the idiot. The Birds were right about him. But Lena lived with the man and she's always respected me for the most part. Besides I like the way she grieves. Tell the story but hold the tears. Unlike my mother who was always crying, grieving the early passing of her sister, grieving the early passing of my father and everything in between. Cry at the drop of the hat. God, I hated when she cried.

I overheard the preacher say she was crying 'cause she had nobody to drink with anymore. Whatever, grieved herself to an early grave. I felt correct in my decision not to attend her funeral. I also felt inclined to change my name. Actually to shorten it from Snookee to Snooky. This symbolized my disassociation from her.

43

God rest her soul. Now Daddy, when he was working, was a butcher. He understood the power that butchers have and my mother never respected the status of his calling. Some say Daddy had a sickness but he never seemed that way to me.

Loved trains. He'd say, "Multiply the mass of a train by its length and what do you get? An insignificant number." He'd laugh in a low rumble. Taught me how to be a man too. "Never cry, keep your knives sharp and follow family tradition." I didn't even cry at his funeral.

The waitress sets down three Styrofoam plates of steaming comida and I unroll the paper towel to get at the metal fork and start to eat. But I keep poking holes in the plate and I look over at Little Joe and he's poking holes too.

Lena looks up from her egg, tilts her head and looks down the aisle at the waitress who's got her back to us. Real loud Lena says, "Your plates aint holding up." Her teeth are all crooked and yellow, stained I guess from smoking.

"Range and Animal Science," Little Joe says. "I'll study that."

Lena rolls her eyes. The waitress gives a look. Lena looks at me and says, "So I asked Mole, well, what's your name Mexican. He says, 'Mole.' And I say 'You mean your name is gravy?'" She giggles then stares at the framed velvet matador on the wall. "He really wanted to marry me." She fiddles with her eggs and stuffs a piece of bacon into her mouth, crunching it real good. "He'd always say, 'I'm going to get some work today.' He'd fool ya. You'd think he really was but he never did. He'd say, 'I aint gonna let winter catch me.' And then in spring he'd say, 'Time to get some work.'"

Lena looks out the window. She rubs her eye and her mascara smears. "I wish it was spring time."

In walks the preacher with his wife. He looks over at us, but his wife looks straight ahead keeping her head straight in the air, pushing her little bun of silver hair up. Closet drunk.

44

Bad reflection on the clergy. Honey they call her. Not too sweet if you ask me. Seems like a preacher's wife would want to be extra sweet. I've bagged her groceries, walked them out, set them in the trunk nice and straight and never even got the time of day from her.

"I could be a doctor in seven years," Little Joe says.

Lena nods then shakes her finger in the air. "I'd say, 'Mole today you and me's gonna quit drinkin'. And he'd look at me and say in his low voice, 'Quit? Why quit?' Once he punched me so hard I had to go to the hospital. Thought my liver was going to pop out." She looked at the empty hat rack. "It's hard to believe he's not in this world anymore."

The pain moves down my bowels and I feel like I got to go.

"Maria went to Houston," I say.

"No, she didn't," Lena says.

"Yes, she did. Took the bus."

Tall fellow with a white shirt walks into the restaurant and takes his hat off. He hooks it on the empty rack and looks around then walks over to the counter and sits down. You can tell he's from out of town.

Lena picks up the knife and rubs the blade. "Strange the way Mole died. Seems strange, don't it, Snooky?"

"Huh?" I say. I was listening to a fly buzz in the window.

"Coroner's report say he was cut up like a side of beef," Lena says.

"Nope, side of beef hadn't been cut yet. It's been sawed in half after the kill floor. Then you hang it and age it in the reefer," I say. "Later comes the butchering."

"You know all about cold slabs, doncha?" Lena says.

"I know enough to tell you a side of beef aint been cut yet."

She puts the knife down then starts to tear up. "Mole liked to lay near the railroad tracks on cold days with his big black coat on. I'd walk out to him and say, 'Mole, snows coming.' And Mole, 'Bury me in the backyard.' And I say what and he says, 'Bury me in the backyard and play the Mexican National Anthem.'"

Lena sniffles and looks at the new guy sipping his coffee at the counter. Little Joe raises his head. "I'd be known as Doctor Little Joe."

Lena looks at Little Joe then says, "I heard the manager of the Food Bucket died mysteriously."

"Disrespectful alcoholic," I say. "That's what happens to them."

She tears up again. "Mole was a klutz. Break everything he touched. I'd tell him, 'Don't touch me, I don't want to get broke.'" She collects the loose clumps of eggs with her fork then assembles a small mountain with them in the middle of her plate. She wrinkles her nose and says, "The wheels of his lawnmower fell off once when he was cutting the grass around his mother's grave. I think he gave up when she died. I think I've given up too," she says, looking across the aisle at a broken chair. "Sometimes I iron a blouse, three or four times you know, trying to get the creases just right and then hold it up on a hanger and look at it and wonder, who's going to wear it? I don't even want a body sometimes."

Lena slowly lifts her head up and stares at the ceiling where the tiles are caved in. "Maybe I should've married him."

My hands are under the table fishing for wads of gum. I feel the ache.

"I try to do what's right," Lena says staring at me, but it's like she doesn't see me. "Person does the things they don't want to do. That's what St Paul says somewhere in the Bible. I go into the Chaparral, that's the only bar me and Mole ever went to, we never bar-hopped. I order a Pepsi-Cola and then another and you know there's only so much Pepsi-Cola you can drink. Then I'll say to Tiffany, 'Oh give me a beer.' Next thing I know I've had four or five."

Lena sips her coffee and says, "I aint had a drink since he died."

"What?"

"I stopped drinking," Lena says.

"That's why the birds aint been singing your name," I say.

"What?" Lena asks.

I don't say nothing. I watch Little Joe push his plate of eggs away. He presses his lips together then rubs his thin mustache. His lazy eye wanders into the distance. "Mole drank vodka."

Outside the sun's so hot I can hear my skin moles screaming and in the trees I can see the mulberries hanging heavy in clusters.

"You need to be dropped off somewhere, Snooky?" Little Joe asks.

"No. I'm going to climb the hill and listen to the birds," I say. "Bye Lena." But she just looks at me.

The police took my driver's license away awhile back. I guess I drive like those kamikaze birds. If you study them they are a lot like us. Get up, fly around, eat, drink, yell, fly around some more and die. It's kinda like watching yourself.

I walk down the street and see the new guy in his Crown Vic with his hat off at the stop sign. I yell over at him, "Hey mister!" He turns his head and I raise my hat and put it back down. He looks at me mean, and I see his badge this time.

They're running a special on brisket at the Food Bucket. I go there where it's cool and check it out. I grab a bottle of Sotol and then walk over to the meat department rubbing the back of my neck. Some of the brisket looks bad judging by the gray around the edges. Tricky butchers will couple nice fresh cuts in the same package as your less desirable meat. If a person aint paying attention, they'll end up sorry.

I pass the hardware store and see the preacher. He's walking out with a shovel and a bag of fertilizer. Honey is by his side. "Hey preacher," I say. "Watch out for them birds." He looks at me and keeps walking.

Up on the hill where Maria and I used to go, I sit down in the loose dirt near the plastic flowers I planted shortly after she departed. They're starting to fade. I look up into the trees. Sure enough, the birds are having a party. A long slug of Sotol makes me feel like a party too. Then I take another. A bird falls out of the tree. It bounces on the ground. I want to run over and help it but I don't. I just watch it spasm in the dirt. Then I hear the other birds sing, "Honey, Honey." I think good, I never seen a preacher grieve before. But then I listen a little closer. They're singing, "Snooky, Snooky."

A New Country

"Wait," the clerk said at check-out. His dark eyes gleamed and the knot in his tie was perfect.

"What is it, speak up," said the man, holding the handle of his suitcase.

"You've left your pen, sir." The clerk offered up a green and white hotel pen.

"Aw, hell. I sure did. Why do you suppose I did that?"

The clerk shrugged then smiled and held the pen out like a prize. At the counter, in the lobby on a Saturday morning in downtown Atlanta, their eyes met.

"I don't want it back, get it?"

The clerk stroked his thin mustache. His head wagged left then right. "Yes," he said. "You don't want the complimentary pen."

"No. I don't want the complimentary pen."

The man turned and walked through the lobby and out the revolving door.

A city bus passed blowing black smoke and a pigeon flew over the man's head. He stopped and lit a cigarette. Newspapers whirled in the wind and steam puffed from a grated storm drain. Next to his foot at the crosswalk a green and white hotel pen lay crushed in the crease of the sidewalk.

Human Potential

Jim lit a cigarette, took a drag and then laid it on the edge of the plywood table where he worked the dough for the next day. He looked out the kitchen service window, past the counter and through the window. Cars whooshed by on Second Street.

"I'm going home now," Gloria said. Her mascara was smeared. She shook the net loose from her hair and looked at him. "Do you want pork chops tonight?"

"Whatever," Jim said, not looking up. He studied the stringy dough on the table as he took another drag of the cigarette. The afternoon sun poured through the drive-up window and formed a trapezoid of light on the kitchen wall where the big tongs hung.

Gloria picked up her purse, the mail and the stale donuts. She walked through the back door and down the alley dropping the donuts in the dumpster. She looked back at the donut shop, paused, then turned and walked to her car.

The front door chime rang.

"We're just about closed," Jim called out through the service window.

"Well, are you open or just about open," the Kid said, walking in. The sleeves of his white T-shirt were rolled and a fat zircon hung in one lobe. His hair was greased back and a collection of thin whiskers grew on his chin. His companion smacked glossy lips, tapped her pumps then stuck her thumbs along the waistline of her jeans.

"What do you want?" Jim asked, standing at the kitchen

doorway. He wiped his hands with a towel that hung from his pants under a stained white apron.

"We want a steak," the Kid said. "What do you think we want old man?"

Jim looked at the Kid.

The Kid looked at his girlfriend and then back at Jim.

"Fresh donuts. That's what we want," the Kid said. He cocked his jaw and shook his head.

"Nobody has fresh donuts in the afternoon," Jim said.

"Nobody?" The Kid held his mouth open. "What kind of donut man are you?"

Jim watched the Kid's eyes roam then lock on the cash register.

"This is Gloria's Custom Donuts. If you come back tomorrow morning we'll have fresh donuts," Jim said.

"Tomorrow," the Kid said. "Did you hear that Marci? Tomorrow he's going to have fresh donuts."

Marci nodded her head. She blew a bubble. Then it popped.

The Kid walked back to the front door and flipped the 'Open' sign to 'Closed'.

"Old man," the Kid said. "We need fresh donuts – now." The Kid ran his fingers through his hair then nodded to Marci. She pulled a revolver from her back pocket.

"Now Marci here," the Kid started, "is a good shot. And she likes donuts. So," his voice slowed, "you go on back to the kitchen and make some fresh donuts." Then he smiled and said, "Got it?"

Jim looked down at the black grip of his pistol showing underneath a stack of newspaper. He looked up at Marci and the gun, then turned, stepped toward the kitchen, and stopped.

"I didn't tell you to stop," the Kid said.

"What kind of donuts do you want?" Jim asked with his

back to them.

"Oh, that's a good question and considerate of you," the Kid said. "Don't you think that was considerate of him, Marci?"

Marci looked out the window.

"I think we should have one of each," the Kid said. "Don't you Marci?" he asked.

"Move," Marci said to Jim.

Jim pulled an earlobe with his fingers.

The Kid tapped Jim on the shoulder.

"Old man. Don't get any ideas. Marci needs her donuts. They're important," the Kid said. "It's a goal we can cross off. Get your mind right. You like to get your mind right, don't you?"

Jim walked to the dough table. He laid out a sheet of wax paper, then turned the knob on the grease pot.

"Do you mind if I smoke?" Jim asked.

"Yes, as a matter of fact we do mind," the Kid said. He looked at Marci then looked at Jim.

"Smoking is unhealthy," the Kid said. "It's one of your bad habits."

"Your name?" Marci asked Jim.

"My name?" Jim cocked an eyebrow. "My name is Jim Baland."

"Jim Baland," Marci repeated.

"Jim Baland," the Kid said.

"Jim Baland," Jim said.

"Hey, Jim Baland, what do you know?" the Kid said.

Jim Baland almost smiled.

"They say that victims should always introduce themselves to their assaulters," the Kid said. "The familiarity of a name reduces tension. You failed to do that Jim Baland."

The Kid looked at Marci then back at Jim.

"Do you feel enlightened now, Jim Baland?" the Kid asked.

The grease in the fryer popped and Jim looked at the Kid then tapped the temperature gauge. He pressed the cutter into the dough and formed long-johns. He reached for the big tongs, then squeezed and dropped the long-johns into the hot grease.

"I just love the smell of frying donuts," the Kid said. "Don't you, Marci?"

"Is that gun actually loaded?" Jim asked.

Marci pressed the pistol straight out, pointing it at Jim's head.

"Do you actually want to find out?" the Kid asked.

Marci whirled and fired a bullet into a sack of flour a foot from the Kid. A cloud of white puffed into the air.

"Goddam, Marci," said the Kid.

"Goddam," said Marci.

"What the fuck!" Jim held his arms out. "What is going on?"

"You're supposed to be making donuts, Jim Baland, not questioning reality," the Kid said. "But I give you credit. You should question reality from time to time."

The Kid looked at Marci then said, "If you burn the donuts Jimmy, Marci is going to blow your head off."

Jim flipped the donuts out of the grease and onto the drip pan. Then he filled syringes with goo.

"Look at those donuts, Marci," the Kid said. "Look at them puff up."

The Kid took a bite of the raspberry donut. "Umm, that's not a bad donut, Jimmy. How long you been cooking donuts?" the Kid asked.

"Twenty-three years," Jim said.

"Twenty-three miserable years," the Kid said. "My my my."

"Marci, try this lemon one," the Kid said.

Marci bit it, then spit it out.

"Goddamn," she said.

"Marci doesn't like that one," the Kid said.

"Try the vanilla," the Kid said.

Marci bit and spit it at the feet of Jim Baland.

"Well I guess Marci doesn't like your donuts," the Kid said. "What's wrong with your donuts, Jimmy?"

"I wouldn't know," Jim said. "Haven't had one in seven years."

"Marci, did you hear what I heard?" the Kid asked.

Marci rolled her eyes.

"I was afraid I'd get fat," Jim said.

"You're fat anyway," the Kid said.

Jim looked down at the donuts on the floor.

"Do you have a wife, Jimmy?"

"Yes."

"When was the last time you made love to her?"

"I don't remember."

"You don't remember?" the Kid asked. "Do you have children?"

Jim wiped his forehead with a towel.

"You haven't answered my question, Jimmy," the Kid said.

"I have a son," Jim said.

"A son? What's his name? What's he do?"

"His name is Rueben and he lives in Austin at the State School of ..."

"For what?" the Kid asked. "For the retarded? The state school for the retarded?" The Kid looked at Marci.

"Autism," Jim said.

"Autism," the Kid said. "So your kid's stupid, huh?"

"Not stupid, autistic."

"Whatever," the Kid said. "When was the last time you spoke to him?"

Jim put his hand on his forehead. "I guess a year."

The Kid looked at the grease in the grease pot.

"Seems like a long time not to talk to your flesh and blood, Jimmy."

The Kid looked up, then at the clock on the wall, then at Marci.

"Are you ready to get your mind right, Jim Baland?" the Kid asked.

"What do you mean?" Jim asked.

"What do you think we mean?" the Kid asked then looked at Marci.

Marci lowered her eyes.

"Cash register Jimmy, go," the Kid said.

Jim opened the cash register and counted the bills. The Kid grabbed the wad of money. Then he pushed Jim down on the floor and reached under the cash register and pulled out Jim's .38 Special.

"Why didn't you use this, Jimmy, while you had a chance?" the Kid asked.

Jim stared at the gun.

"Go in there and eat those donuts on the floor. And crawl," the Kid said.

Jim looked out the window.

"Eat the goddamn donuts," the Kid said.

Jim turned his head and looked at the Kid then at Marci.

"No," he said.

The Kid rubbed his hair, and cocked his jaw. Marci cocked the hammer on the pistol.

"Shoot me," Jim said flatly.

"Where, in the foot, in the leg, in the heart?" the Kid asked.

"Shoot me dead," Jim said. "Shoot me in the heart. I'm ready."

"Just like that you're ready to die? What the fuck is wrong with you?"

"I've been ready."

"You been ready? What about your wife, your kid, this

55

goddam business. We're talking about human potential, Jimmy! You just gonna let it go and die?"

"Yes."

"And you want Marci to do your dirty work?"

"Why not? She's got the gun."

"Are you getting smart with me? Here you are with three minutes left in your miserable life and now you're getting smart?"

"Why not?"

The Kid turned and looked at Marci. He relaxed his jaw, bowed his head, rubbed his hair, and raised Jim's pistol in the air. He opened his mouth, and closed it. He looked around the donut kitchen.

"Come on, we're finished," the Kid said.

Marci looked at Jim.

"We're done – come on," the Kid flipped open Jim's .38 Special, stuffed the bullets in his pants and tossed the pistol on the floor. Then he took the wad of money and threw it at Jim.

"I should keep it," the Kid said.

Marci took another look at Jim and then followed the Kid out the front door.

They jumped in the car, drove to the light and turned left on Oak Street. The Kid lit a cigarette.

"Who's next?" he asked.

Marci opened the glove box and pulled out some papers. "A guy named Magnus at Bill's Furniture Store on Argosy. They close at five." She stuck a piece of gum in her mouth and looked out the window.

"I'm going in as the same punk," the Kid said.

He tapped his ashes out the window.

"I think I'll wear a long dress for Magnus."

"No. Keep the jeans – girl, they're sexy."

"I'll wear what I want."

The Kid glanced at her, flicked his cigarette and drummed

his hands on the steering wheel.

"If we do three more today, I'll buy you that leather lingerie you wanted."

"I don't want it, you want it," Marci said.

"Whatever." He rubbed his jaw. "What do we know about this Magnus fellow?"

Marci watched a pigeon fly off a rooftop.

The Kid adjusted the rear view mirror. "Oh, better call Ms. Baland and tell her the job's done."

Marci said, "I think we overdid it," She looked at the Kid. "I got a feeling something happened. I got a feeling something's not right with Jim Baland. What if he's dead?"

"Dead? His wife signed the release, she ordered it – we're covered, don't worry," the Kid said. "Front office has it under control. They've been doing this in California for years."

"I don't like this. It's mean," she said. "I'm not mean by nature. You might be. I'd rather be in Phase II."

"Takes much more experience in Phase II," the Kid said. "Lifting those people up after they've been pummeled. Delicate. But when they finish the training they come out stronger, clear. Look at Yuri in the front office, all that bling and the Mercedes. Ever seen anybody more clear?"

Nothing Really Ordinary

I had just begun the interview with Billie Lee Dankowski but had already lost control. A familiar feeling. Control left me long ago: the divorce, the collapse of my business, too many bars and restaurants, especially bars. I looked at Billie Lee. She had it together. Still felt things. Everything mattered. Now it was midnight and tomorrow's deadline must've been written all over my face.

"That's the difference between newspapers and magazines," she grinned.

Outside, lightning bolts inside mushroom clouds lit the night sky. Thunder pounded. Lights flickered. A red-bearded man burst through the door into the strobing light then tripped and slid across the floor.

"I'm looking for Billie Lee Dankowski," he said now, standing to his feet and brushing himself off. His wet hair was matted against his head.

"I'm she."

Billie Lee's professional: confident, drove out from Austin, was teaching a four-day writers course.

The man in blue Dickies work pants and matching shirt nodded, took his hands out of his pockets.

"Billie Lee Dankowski, how do you do? I'm Jackson Auberge." He shook her hand then lifted his finger in the air. "I've something for you."

Billie Lee watched Auberge walk back out the door then looked down and adjusted the yellow flower in her lapel. She cleared her throat, "Anyway, the first assignment I gave my students was to write a thousand words on anything they wanted," she said with her perpetual smile, the lights for the moment, stable. She took a drag from an e-cig and exhaled preposterously, loosening a flume of blue smoke. "One story stood out."

"Oh," I said.

"You know there's nothing really ordinary in life."

"No?"

"Take a guy like you, stuck in the mundane as if the mundane actually existed." She cocked her head, the smile again creeping across her face. "Am I right?"

I could feel my face redden, the worm of inspection slithering through my thoughts. Her probing silhouette perched now straining at my mundaneness, her long legs and penetrating eyes stirring in me a low-boil.

"See the rain. Feel it. Taste it. Smell it. Witness wetness. Actualize. Is that your reference?" I asked with a hint of sarcasm.

"Nice," she said. She looked out the window, then circled her lips deftly with her pinky. "So this guy's six-year-old daughter stopped talking."

"Stopped?" I asked, thinking about my own daughter.

"Wrote she was different from his other children, always had been. Full of life then stopped saying anything at all."

"Nothing?"

"Mute. Like she'd seen too much."

"Most times I feel there's not enough."

"Oh, it's all out there, darling." She said it with gusto like life at the edge of muteness was the place to be.

Jackson Auberge pushed through the door again cradling a wood coffin under his arm, like Queequeg's casket in 'Moby Dick' – but miniature. He kneeled down and opened the box. A violin. He tucked it under his beard and plucked.

"Needs tuning," Auberge declared. He feathered the strings with the bow then handed it to Billie Lee. "I want you to give it to Willie."

Billie Lee had just finished a book on the life of Willie Nelson. She can tell you about his DJ days in Portland, his first night playing at the Panther Hall Ballroom in Ft. Worth, and his disappearance in 2008.

Billie Lee studied the instrument; crusty, Italian. A Stradivari.

"It's extraordinary," she said. "But I think you should keep it. He won't accept this. Maybe give it to his church in Abbott. Go on a Sunday, he might be there."

Something rattled inside the violin.

"Yucca seed. Helps with the vibes," he said. "Had snake rattles but heard Willie was an activist." Auberge leaned back in his chair and pulled his beard. He looked at Billie Lee. "Precious aint it? The moment and all. Hellfire." He looked out the window into the rain. "Marfa in a night storm trying to give away a Stradivari." He looked pleased with the situation then looked at the clock. "Better get back to Van Horn. Told the ole lady I'd be home before the sun come up." He put the violin back in the case.

Outside, lightning lit up Auberge's copper-colored 1968 Dodge Charger. "Runs on nitro. She'll do two hundert," he shouted through the window and the Charger rumbled to the stop sign.

Billie Lee and I stood in the rain leaning toward each other. Our shoulders touched. We watched Jackson Auberge roar into the stream of lights, down the highway, steel steered by man-electric pulled along in the flat plateau of darkness.

Billie Lee looked at the neon of the newspaper office, then at the sky, then at me.

"Are we done?" she asked.

I reached through the raindrops and pulled her to me. Her warm wet body fueled the wound up traffic in my brain. I planted my lips on hers. She raised her arms and pushed off.

"There's a moment to every beginning," she said, still back-pedaling, "and this aint one of them." Billie Lee Dankowski took one more look at me, disgust or amusement I could not tell, then turned and walked away, her heels clicking, popping, against the wet pavement.

I drove home that night down the two-lane highway at 3AM thinking about her words. "Stuck in the mundane." I spoke it out loud. A lightning bolt flashed behind me and I watched it backlight a giant parallelogram of rain through the rear-view mirror. I'll lasso the lightning, I thought. I'll give voice to the mute. I'll grow yellow flowers. The ground underneath the truck hummed, humming me closer to the stars ahead, my apartment, my bed, a Xanax. I flicked the radio on. I listened for a few seconds then turned it off. I made a U-turn. I pushed on the gas. Back down the mountain. The lightning crackled. Thunder pounded. I rolled the window down and the rain swooshed in.

Foucault Hill

The beep baa bops and I like "Yeah," and Sonny Wax say, "Do you know I'm Jewish?" I say "Fuck – what it matter? You want some raw dog?"

There's silence then Sonny say, "Yes."

I meet Sonny at the Flipjack. Connie the bitch, flipping. She starts to sing and it's like, "I'm not waiting for you bitch, I'm getting on with Sonny Wax."

We order a Martini. Everybody here is quilt bag but I'm not into it, in fact I really haven't faced the whole total fucking organic goddam truth, I mean, father don't know. Or I don't think he know. Or maybe I don't know him. He raised me: "Peter it's four – homework."

One day I burned the book of French existentialists. "Peter why?" he asked when he saw the blackened remnants laying on the patio bricks. Uh, like dyslexia and reading don't mix? He never got that. "I can't read, father." I clear my throat. "Being aware of one's life, one's revolt, one's freedom, and to the maximum, is living and to the maximum," I said. "Sartre."

"Camus," he corrected and walked away.

Now I tell Sonny he's got five minutes to finish and take me.

He's wearing a kasha. What up with that?

A white Daimler cabriolet drives by. It's Morgan, of course, his scarf is flying, white hat, red sash, and the blackest skin you ever seen. He's like anti-poverty, or dark matter or fuck I don't know.

I sell blunt, hustle, do tours at the wharf; cruise near the telescopes hawking Alcatraz, extended stays, and BJs. I'm an inventor too. Patenting the Poly Hole – for Mollies that got too much. They adjust the holes, like, match crevices, then rotate.

"Goddamn you are stupid you know that?" I tell Sonny Wax. "I'm outta here, bitch." Sonny just looks at me and Connie, she's like, "Here he go, look at that man, is that a man, squeeze that onion for me," she says from behind the counter.

I'm a hot head and the lightest black man you'll ever see. Most of the time I pass. My sperm won the 10 inch dash up the vaginal canal. Ever seen a champion black swimmer? No. Outswam the ghetto. Raised in a Victorian by a white man. Joelson Scarpatti.

I catch the 44 and head to Lulu's. Sylvester's on the cell and we line up some shit then I call Stevie for raw dog at Sofi's. A jet rumbles in the clouds. My boner's thrusting.

Last month a man got murdered right in front of me. On the 67. Shot dead with a pistol. Instant, I mean that nigga didn't suffer.

I don't suffer no more myself, I am that I am that I am, I keep telling myself, like Popeye. It's a philosophy, father would agree. Listen I'm going to tell you something. I hold the franchise. Spinning with no stop, flowing. Like everything down for me. Finally fucking finally. I haven't had a setback in months.

I run into Boney M at the stop. He tells me about some eggrolls who got some shit on a sailboat at Horseshoe Bay. I postpone my plans and catch the ferry to Sausalito. I'm walking up the tunnel and then into the marina. Sure enough there's the blue hulled boat and a slanty with a black eye patch comes out to meet me.

Ran this shit from Thailand?

Yes, just want expenses.

How much is that?

Two thousand a kilo.

You gotta be joking? It's 800 for Mexican, Humboldt's 18.

But this Thai stick, very special.

I look at one-eye then look up at the Golden Gate. Cars clatter over loose plate. A breeze blows in from the Pacific. It's like I'm living this enchanted life.

Two thousand but you got to deliver.

You crazy?

No, I'm happy. You go anal?

His good eye blinks.

No.

Well if you want your money, deliver to this address. I hand him the address written on a piece of paper. Take a cab.

Cab with ten kilo?

Suitcase, I say. Wrap the shit in a towel soaked in coke-cola. Look, Tuesday afternoon – dig?

I'm up on 101, walking the Golden Gate back to the city. Twenty G by Tuesday afternoon, I can do it. I loosen my scarf and take it all in, smelling the fog and listening to the click-clack of the loose plate.

I catch the 67 and get out at the Ferry Building. Sofi calls. Lulu's in the tank, again. I feel it between my legs. My mind flashes through the Book of Cock. What about the myth of the Haight: Foucault of Buena Vista Park? Hear he knows the territory, makes it special, if you can find him.

Morgan had him. Say he's the best, Sonny Wax agreed. Sonny know. Got a PhD. Dr Sonny some call'em. Psychiatrist. Told me once I had to "reconcile" the fact that father was not my biological. "Things could happen," he said. "Bizarre things – this from the lips of a Jewish queen."

"Scream" I said and he said "Howl. Very good Peter – Allen Ginsberg."

I saw Pop at the park once. He looked surprised, waved, "Peter, dinner at seven." There was grass in his hair.

I walk up Foucault Hill and feel the energy. It's coming from the fog, low and easy to catch. When I get to the bench this Filipino queer shows up and I'm like trying to shoe him off. "Get the fuck away. I set on who I want."

Product

I stepped off the 26 and walked toward the surf, through the sand, peeling off clothes, dodging fat bankers from New York, lawyers from Minnesota. The jeans drop and now I'm in my green Speedo, no longer part of the daily change but permanently attached. I march on toward water. Showers – you have to be ready. Hygiene's important, and when you're living out of a '91 Camry, essential. Every little step toward clean counts. The more soap, the easier it is to live in the grunge of the universe, play the ponies and take on ventures. I like to step out of the cascade of city water, towel off in the sun, admire my parking space and think: I'm clean.

I torqued the shampoo then returned a call to Louie Mavens down in Opa Locka. Mavens had a deal cooking with a shrimper who had a load of dope. Wanted me to drive to Flamingo, the end of the road in the Everglades, rent a houseboat like a tourist and run out to Florida Bay to rendezvous with his friend.

"Louie, one more thing. My Camry's dead. I need wheels for Flamingo."

"Jack an SUV – you need something big," Louie said.

"Let me use your Jag."

"Sal says you're the right man but I'm beginning to wonder."

"Sal set this up?" I asked.

"Got a van you can have. Meet me at Fidel's on the river at three."

"Sal, huh? OK. I'll be there. Ricky, my boy too."

Ricky called them galaxies, phosphorescent boils between the breakers, schools of shrimp giving off green sparkle in the dark. We'd pull in our throw nets under the Brickell Avenue Bridge, on those rare nights his mother entrusted him with me, make a fire and boil our booty under the moon, smelling the sea and listening to the click-clack of the cars across the iron. I told him shrimp traveled on the surface at night to navigate by the stars like the rusty freighters that passed occasionally under the bridge. I wanted him to know these things, not just the hygiene of the burbs, and that's why I got the idea to bring him to Flamingo. Of course I had to get it by his mother.

"Susan Marie Knotwood?"

"I told you to never call me that. What do you want?"

"Can Ricky come out and play?"

"A child with a child?"

"Fishing. Can I pick him up or not?"

She used to call me Rick. I go by Richard now. We tried to make a go of it. Maybe we gave up too soon. Stayed out of prison at least. I never could give up the biz. Ran a chemical business front. Not what you think; light metals primarily, zinc, aluminum – food grade for the pet industry, dog food additives. Keeps them healthy. Yeah OK so if they shit on your lawn, you got some blue-white in the soil. No biggee, right? Better than lead.

"Assertive these days," she says finally. "Have him back by Sunday, no later than seven."

At Fidel's, Louie gave me the keys and coordinates. I drank a Bud, Ricky, Mountain Dew. I looked at the freighter docked across the river. I thought about my chances. I thought about Sal and the money I owed him; ten grand and growing five per cent a week. I popped three beans.

Ricky and I drove south out of Miami, past the Tamiami Trail, past the row of Wackenhut prisons.

"Did Grandpa go to prison?" Ricky asked as he watched the metro glide along the raised tracks, his hair curly with the morning fog.

"Fifteen years."

"Why did he die?"

"He gave up," I said. "Don't you ever give up."

"Give up what?"

I looked out beyond the sea of sawgrass wondering how to explain what the what was.

"I thought Grandpa died in the glades?" Ricky asked.

"You can die more than once," I said. "There's a kind of death that's not final."

We let go the mooring lines at noon that day in a houseboat named Redfish and chugged through the tannin water of the everglades. Ricky counted alligators. Eight hours and a few snook later we crossed Little Shark River into Ponce de Leon Bay. The motor wheezed as we passed the mangrove islands in the late afternoon. The air was hot and thick and white herons floated ahead and occasionally the gray fins of a dolphin cut the surface following us in the wake. I studied the chart as Ricky steered toward the open water of Florida Bay.

"Why can't we go fishing every day?"

"What about school?" I asked. "You don't want to end up like me, do you? See that piling, steer toward it."

"Why?"

"'Cause we're meeting some people there tonight."

"There are other people out here?"

We dropped anchor 100 yards offshore. In the west the sun glowed red, then melted into the sea. We fried the snook.

"I love you son," I said, suddenly half-calm with myself.

"I love you too, Dad."

"I love you more than all the stars in the sky," I said looking into his fresh eyes, vice-less orbs, at the beginning of the whole thing. "I love your chances. You're going to knock it out of the park someday."

"You're going to bust it up too, Dad," Ricky said.

Ricky turned in and I stood on deck in the moonlight with the wind blowing, a cold shiver in my veins, a pang of guilt knotting in my gut. Did I need a buzz to tell my son I loved him? Marlboro smoke curled in my lungs. What is the what? I took another shot of Jack then heard the putter of a diesel. I looked for running lights but saw only the yellow glow of Key West.

No choice, I told myself, pull this gig and pay the vig, then a nice long shower.

Last time I was really clean the Florida penal system offered to train me. Night school, they called it, after my ten in Campbell Soup's tomato fields. It was a chance to get legit, clean you might say, and the money, according to the warden, was in electronics but I took biology and a course in business. I learned about evolution, mass extinctions, supply and demand and how laws protect businesses like Pfizer, Bayer and Energy Transfer.

The moonlight caught the hull of a shrimp boat as it cut through the chop. It slowed and a shadow appeared on deck wearing farmer johns, white rubber boots and a scraggly beard.

"You wanna throw me a line?" he asked.

I tossed him the white nylon and he married up.

"You the only one on board?" he asked.

"My son's here."

"Where's he at?"

"Sleeping."

"Bring him out."

"What the hell for? He's ten years old."

The skipper looked at me then back at the fantail. Nets swung from the rigging, the wind gusting. Another figure

69

appeared, dark-skinned, dark-clothed, bearded with a knife strapped to his leg.

"You know anything?" the skipper asked.

"Flim-flam," I said. That's the code.

"Alright Flim-flam. Gonna swing some dope on your boat. It's a ton so she'll list, where you want it?"

I point to the afterdeck.

"Don't you want it against the wheel house?"

"No."

He signaled to the gypsy. The winch motor whined. The cargo hook floated down into the hatch of the shrimp boat.

"You got my money?" the skipper asked.

I lift the brown envelope from my pocket.

"How much?"

"I just deliver."

He looked at me. The gypsy winched up the bale of dope and it hung over the hatch.

"You mind if I come aboard?" the skipper asked.

"Not until the dope lands," I said.

"You're not a very trusting man now are you?"

"Following orders, you might say."

"You might say, huh?"

He motioned to the gypsy and the winch whined again. The dope swung in the air, half lit by the moon. A seagull flew low and cawed. I caught the guy line and pulled the boom across the decks.

"I'll take the envelope now," the skipper said.

I leaned over the gunwale and handed him the money.

He grabbed it and counted. Ricky walked out on deck and looked at the dope hanging in the air.

"What's that, Daddy?"

"What's that, Daddy?" the skipper mimed, laughing. He pulled a bottle from his pocket and swigged it. "What's that

Daddy?" he mimed again, then signaled the gypsy and the bale dropped to the deck.

The way he sucked on the bottle, the larynx ratcheting under the skin of the throat, the eyes. I knew the look. It was my father. It was me. It was every man steering toward second death, the finale. I pulled the Jack out of my pocket, then the tweek and tossed them in the drink. They whirled in an eddy.

"That's product, son," I said.

"Product?" Ricky asked. His mother's piercing blue eyes collided with mine.

The skipper looked at us. A wave broke between the boats and water gushed on the decks.

"It's been a pleasure doing business with you Flim-flam." He fired up the diesel and threw back the line. The shrimp boat gurgled, then motored away across the dark building sea.

"Product huh, Dad?" Ricky asked. "What do they use this product for?" I said something about distorting minds and then he asked what the mind is and I says it's your brain and everything you've ever experienced pulsates inside it, like stars in a galaxy and this product turns some stars off. He walked curious around the product. "You're hauling marijuana to pay off your gambling debt, right?"

"Right," I said, and at that moment I knew I was going clean.

Clausen's Farm

We drove deeper into Clausen's farm, the clay rocky road slick from the morning's rain. A sweetness perfumed the desert air, and in the valley below, trees glossy with moisture shrouded the Rio Grande in a serpentine of green.

The steering wheel jiggled as I drove the rent-a-jeep across another cattle guard. Don craned his neck out of the window trying to spot Clausen's alfalfa field. Clausen, a former insurance salesman from Dallas bought hard red land in the Big Bend and had turned farmer. He was hoping to have enough hay to bale by the end of the season but he wasn't so sure anymore.

"Eating me out of house and home," Clausen mumbled. He stood in the cold air and smoked. His blue jeans were creased and the sunglasses snug on his nose mirrored the mountains in Mexico.

Hungry javelinas had found the ordered green rows of his agricultural project along the river, irresistible. We had met him at Cecilia's Store on the river road. He saw our rifles in the back seat and convinced us that thinning out the marauders would be a marked step in the progress of man. Being from Florida, we didn't know much better and didn't need much convincing either, having just been skunked on a deer-hunting trip we shared with a zillion other hunters in the Guadeloupe National Forest.

We had spent two hours filling out forms in the ranger's office. The screechy-voiced guy in line behind us kept talking about his two thousand-dollar infrared scope and how unfair it was to let the bow hunters hunt a week before the bullet guys. Everything was unfair to him; the fee, the long line, the no vehicle zone. Imagine that – he'll have to actually get out of his truck to hunt.

The next morning, I shivered behind my tree in the pre-dawn opening day cold listening to bullets being chambered all around me. I expected to die in the crossfire but luck was with me, not a deer to be seen and we headed south to Texas that afternoon, alive.

Approaching another gate, I drove through a two-lane puddle and high-centered the axle of the Hertz two-wheel drive rent-a-jeep. The tires spun, whining in the still air. The once white jeep sank deeper.

"Call your girlfriend," Don said, referring to my friend Rita who dispatched for a wrecker in Miami.

"That's funny."

"I'd call my wife but she's probably busy."

"You don't have a wife."

"I didn't tell you? I married a Colombiana." He laughed and the rolls of fat on his three hundred pound frame jiggled.

"You been holding out on me," I said. "Did you consummate?"

"Of course not. She's a friend." He looked at me with a quirked eyebrow. "Needs the green card. Sends half of what she makes to Medellin every month."

Tattered white plastic bags caught on a barbed wire fence fluttered in the light wind. I looked out over the desert puddle.

"Come on, this aint Okeechobee. What's a little water to a couple of Florida tipos?"

"Ride on," Don said. His eyes narrowed. Camouflage mascara covered his face and caked on his long lashes. "Pigs-ho."

"They're not pigs. They're javelinas."

"Have a que?"

"Javelinas."

We stepped out of the jeep and stood shin deep in water. A yellow butterfly flapped in the air and landed on the barrel of my rifle. Don tapped his finger in the air gesturing toward the river. Our soaked boots mucked and crunched across the red rocky dirt, piercing the desert silence as the pale orange rays from the late sun spiked behind the mountain peaks.

A coyote appeared from nowhere, fifty yards away and squatted. Don turned and lifted his rifle but the animal vanished.

The sweet smell of alfalfa crossed our path and we marched toward it. We passed through another gate then walked between two trailer homes, the roofs caved in, the rusty sides bent and door-less. We walked across an island of shredding carpet and through patches of purple cactus and legions of tall gray spiny shoots with tiny red flowers that grew between old mattresses and a grayish '71 Grand Prix.

In the east, a nearly full moon glowed between the jagged peaks. Overhead a buzzard circled. Don jerked his barrel up and aimed.

"Don't shoot," I said.

He tapped his thick finger on the stock and glared.

We marched on.

We stopped in front of another cattle guard. 'Lopez' was welded in rusty iron on the center of the gate. "You sure we got the right place?" Don whispered. "The guy's name was Clausen, wasn't it?"

"We got the right place. A long time ago a guy named Lopez owned all the land around here. General López de Santa Anna," I said.

In the distance, just beyond rusting black and red oil drums, the alfalfa patch flaunted a strange green in the dying light and the tractored rows reflected oddly against the wildness of the desert. The plants staggered in height, some

74

stalks without leaves. I chambered a bullet into my 30.06, leveled the barrel atop a cedar fence post and peered through the scope panning the field.

POW, POW, POW! Don's 50 caliber semi-automatic fired. The sulfurous taste of spent gunpowder filled my nostrils and my ears rang as the blasts echoed.

"Colombiana?" I asked.

"Three, I think. Did you?"

"Bonita?"

"Bonita?" Don stared. "What's wrong with you, man? Shoot'em up. The more the merrier, the bigger the better – this is Texas, remember?"

We stood silent in the twilight. The moon climbed aiding the sun's dimming light. Ten more minutes and my scope would be useless. It wasn't an infrared type but still provided plenty of cheat. Down by the river a diesel pump fired up, bellowing black exhaust and sucking stagnant water out of the Rio Grande to irrigate the already soaked alfalfa.

I panned the field again. Nothing. Then a dark image appeared in the crosshairs. It blurred through the barbed wire toward the first row of plants. The animal lowered its snout and began to munch. I fingered the dial on the scope. The magnification pinpointed the head. POW!

We trudged alongside the leaking irrigation pipe that led to the far corner of the alfalfa field. Four javelinas lay dead, one on its side in the wet dirt, head missing, another with half its back and all the choice meat blown off and the other two, too bloody to tell. In the dark beyond the fence the remaining javelinas snorted.

I dropped the rifle and the scope hit a rock. The metallic clang hung in the air as if the earth winced at filtering such blood. I spit, then picked up the rifle and slammed the scope into a rock, smashing the lens.

"What are you doing?" Don asked.

"Nothin'," I said.

I pulled my knife out and sank its sharp tip into the soft belly of the headless javelina, slitting the hide down the inside of the front legs to the anus. I reached my hand into the dead animal and pulled the hot steaming guts out of the cavity.

We fashioned a harness out of a branch and bailing wire. Don dragged the javelinas across the rocky wet dirt while I studied the blood splattered on the ground, following, marching behind with the rifles.

Don stopped. "You drag'em for awhile." He dropped the harness and looked at the carcasses. "You sure we can eat these things? Clausen said they're nasty."

I stared at the slots of his eyes.

"I say leave'em," Don said.

"No!" I said. "We're gonna eat'em – cheeks, ribs, hearts – everything."

I set the thick branch across my shoulders, and with arms spread wide, I dragged the dead stinking animals with the cross-like contraption. Snorting, the other javelinas followed, from the periphery of dark brush watching as I dragged their brothers and sisters over the rocky dirt, in the light of the moon, toward the stuck rent-a-jeep on Clausen's farm.

Dark Energy with Its Foot on the Gas

Stop again. Stop-stop-stop. Dominique say "Daddy, we're not moving." I grin. He grin. I walk the aisle to the bus driver – "Quisiera vamos a Isla Vieques." "Vieques?" the mustached driver say – "Hombre, how much time ju got?"

Segment one of our trip. Hitchhike (don't tell Momma, OK?) – First car stops "like whatup?" Woofers woofing. Shake of the head. "Nobody hitchhike in San Juan. Catcha gua-gua." Woofer man takes us to the stop. The people – these people, these Puerto Ricans buzzing, hot air, hot garbage, feeling this sweat, trying to help us. I mean the peeps are the blood of the land!

"How did the universe start?" Dominique asks. He's five. Curious. "It's not like the A train – Harlem start, Harlem end," I say. No, I'm thinking, boy at my side, pigeons flying, rain falling. We're not in Nueva York. Astronomic skies over Ponchatoula long gone too. Waves in a Van Gogh sky. Small waves. Tiny. Infinitesimal. Motherless and loaded. Big Bang. Gotta catch that ferry – can't this thing go faster?

"Ju got two alternatives; wait for the green bus or walk Fifth Street to Sixty-fifth..." Dominique say walk. We walk. Five hundred degrees and learning new things. No.5 thing learned these people are the blood of the land! No.4 keep walking – "Hey, where the Gua-gua to the Ferry at?" Dangling participle and all dangling. He short-sleeved and dark sucking Marlboro say go this way that way all in PR Spanish and we see the Walgreens – this is Carolina town – cars with a/c, clocks, belle arte, here.

"The universe started with the Big Bang," I say to Dominique and he looks at me. "That's all we got. Prevailing theory. Exploded into being. Like a nervous gun. Boom. Stars. Planets. Some Mercuries, some Earths." Fortified, we walk. Dominique ask, "Why does the ferry float (and not sink)?" "By universal laws but not THE LAW (Big Bang Crazy Dark Energy with Its Foot on the Gas)." Ever-expanding. Accelerating. Walking, nearly a trot, born-again Fajardo sidewalk grandma wants to preach but we already purposed – episodes stretched out over time. Five billion years. Another car stops. "Get in." We get in. Five bucks. Five slides. "Him too?" "UH-huh." Five slide again. Blood of the land. Shotgun man turns, looks. So much can happen. Five seconds. Five years. Takes you places. Five years dark energy defined. Five years sees a lot of distance. Five minutes in a car with Mercury himself? Five more bucks. Each. "Let us out." "No". Five more bucks slide. Shotgun man now with nervous pistol. Five slide again. Five more. Eyelids red half-open half-smile half-demon eye brow quirked "THE LAW" he say – points to the pistol, mouth open, staccato laugh, five slide again, pistol waving driver driving crazy now.

Rubber

Priestly hands folded, tapped, balled into fists then opened again, palms up, myrrh in the air. The pointer of the right hand nervous, beaconing, as if to coax more. Smooth wood, tight grain, lacquered in a sheen of yellow. The lines in his palm faulted in the skin like rivers – stretched, elongated. Again, hands on the wood inside the confessional. How many times had I wondered why my own hands could not be those of a priest?

My name is Weiss, or I should say, my family's European name was Weiss; it's been changed many times. In Romania they called me Yanko, in Queens, Thomas, Thomas Gotti. Before Europe, and long ago, my people came from Rajasthan. Low in the caste, my ancestors held their Hindu fate yet migrated, some east but most went west, across the Tar, the Indus, and through the Khyber Pass. A few settled in Istanbul but many moved on, fully developing our Romani reputation in Constanta. My mother and father were born European Romas, but made it to New York City by shipping out, signing on, as dishwashers aboard the "Queen Elizabeth II" with me in the lee of a sea chest.

I know now a gypsy should not be Catholic, much less a priest. But by way of circumstance our tenement was just down the street from St. Joan of Arc Holy Church of Christ Jesus Our Lord in Queens. I watched them from my perch in the oak tree, the dapper parents with the entourage of frolicking kids dressed in Gap black and white gliding through the doors for the 5 o'clock Saturday mass. I slipped in one day and was immediately ushered to a youth group. To my mother's chagrin I was confirmed in two fast years. The price: reject my Gypsy roots and become part of the Catholic machinery which in turn began the chain of confessions with Father O'Reilly.

Palms down on the wood. Loose skin creased in hanging folds. The skin of an elephant. He'd turn his head, direct an ear, just slightly, waiting for a moment of evidence, then lean in with cupped palms as if waiting for droplets of mercy to fall, to well up and fill the elongated lines with the liquid weight of God's tears.

I practiced when nobody was home, tapping, balling, flattening my hands between the knots in the grain of the wood of the kitchen table, those dark knots like the contusions of Jesus; spikes in the wrists, the feet, the puncture in his side. I avoided touching them, but if penitence mused from the other side, I would lean, assess their soul, as if I could tell, as if the unseen spiritual world opened before me. Then with the power entrusted to me, inch a deft finger to the knot, touch the contusion and soak up the blood of Christ.

Confession.

I killed Father O'Reilly.

It happened in the Bronx, at the old rectory. Candlelight flickered across Melinda's face. A blackened spoon lay next to her on the floor, the box of Blue Diamond matches open, the pistol hot in my hand. She tried to piece together what had happened in the hallway; the smell of sulfur, the thumps of penetrated flesh, the flash of light, bodies pounding the wall, an exchange of yells, words, the knock at the door.

Elephants and rats: they are holy in the Hindu religion. If I'd stayed Hindu, my life – as I think about O'Reilly's clasping hands – would be different now. If my people had stayed in India, and cleaned excrement from the streets giving daily thanks to all of Krishna's 108 gods, maybe my love of a white girl would be just a fold in the universe, close but never known.

To develop my whiteness, I studied Plato, Shakespeare, Sartre. But it was with dubious results – the American mainstream offered me little traction. They harbored a fear of small numbers, I was still outside looking in – a slot akin to a stalled reincarnation, as if Lord Yamaraj, Magistrate of Death, had sniffed out complications in my Hindu roots, reported to the minister of American Culture suggesting my soul was confused and in the midst of crossover. Or perhaps, Plato's machine of trans-migration, perplexed by a soul such as mine, was actually considering annihilation. But more likely, a Purgatory, in the full sense of its medieval roots – a place of both purification and punishment, a place of proximity where distance great and small could not be fathomed and capricious, simple pardons hung in spiritual space, awaiting a mere nod that could make me one of them or no nod at all and forever the black joke.

Now a beam shoots from the New Orleans Harbor Police's flashlight bouncing off blocks of raw rubber in the dock warehouse. Forklifts, slings, cracked windows, chains and chicken bones stage my theft. Hidden in a sea of pallets, I squeeze down the hole in the concrete floor and swing my legs underneath. Like a good gypsy I know the ins and outs. Below the dock, my foothold fails. I fall and loose the raft line, sliding down the piling, slamming against the stringers, twisting my ankle as it jacks past a junction of steel rods. I hug the creosoted pole as spiny black barnacles score my skin and then I lurch to a stop. My feet dangle inches above the Mississippi River. The half-loaded raft, listing with rubber loot, shoots away without me in the hard bubbling current.

Two days ago the "Sucidava", a Romanian ship, arrived from Bangkok with 1,001.25 metric tons of rubber. I know because I work this dock. I'm a checker – check off this load, check off that load. Longshoring doesn't pay well, but importing... well, it's in the blood and by now second nature. It works like this: after the last shift I sneak back to the Governor Nichols Wharf, muscle the marked forty-pound rubber blocks to the hole in the dock warehouse floor and drop stow it on the plywood deck of the makeshift raft. Then I float down to the abandoned Poland Street Wharf, load my van and head for Treme. We cut the blocks there. The product is consistently packaged in the 'Phuket Gazette'. Sometimes I wish I could read Thai, find out what's happening along the Gulf of Siam, read the police blotter, see if I recognize any Romi names.

It all started in Brooklyn, Pier One. The union business agent's name was Michaels, a parishioner of Father O'Reilly's. At 16 I had a union card, caught on fast and by 17, I was a checker and soon very much part of the operation and for the first time in my life, acknowledged. It helped that I spoke Romanian and the tobacco exports from Turkey often travelled on freighters flying the Romanian flag. I make contact with the Captain, he hands me a stowage plan so I know where to look for the special marks on the hog sheds; blue moons, yellow scorpions, black clinched fists, a little diversion in the warehouse, our own delivery trucks and everybody's happy, especially the junkies.

Romanian ships were a favorite at the local. Their government contracted to build a hundred ships of the same Soviet design, a design from the 1950s, inefficient, wings so deep you need a machine in the hold to get a square stow. And the cargo gear? A sputtering joke, always breaking down, you can count on it – at a standby rate of $21.75 an hour. Add the basket of maladies they rendered: drunk captains, sailors with bleeding eyes demanding prostitutes, fortune tellers and gifts occasionally, canned codfish livers, Bulgarian cigarettes, Cuban cigars, and of course the more interesting contraband: uncut heroin – what's not to like?

I first became aware of what I might call the "gypsy spirit" as I leaned against the hatch coaming of a Romanian ship called the "Draganesti." A stiff breeze blew out of the Narrows but I smelled Russians, vodka-breathed, and un-bathed. How should I know this? Were they the ones who ordered cheap aluminum wire for the electrical system instead of copper – to pocket a few rubles?

I heard the groans, as I ate my pumpernickel, groans of dying Romanians, the stench of blackened flesh, ships aflame, sinking, distilled in green waters. This power wiggles like a worm inside me, slimed with the elements of cavernous deeds. I told O'Reilly about these glimpses, but he only wrinkled his nose, quirked an eyebrow and said in his sing-song Cork accent, "But are you hungry for God's love, Thomas?"

God's love? I'm a funk of past lives. How could any god string this thing I am? Fate, destiny, re-meated: I roar out against it. Why not a butterfly? Why not a snake?

"But, but, but," I would struggle to get the words out. "I can see things, even about you." And Father O'Reilly would stare, his eye twitching.

He could've been a Wall Streeter, but his feigned priestly obedience to spirit actualized his evil with far more flair. And through the nests of his psyche, foulness was freed – was I the only one who saw it? Father to Father confessions I suggested to him one evening, priest to priest, parity, fairness, absorption into the universal – we are all one. He exploded in Irish rage.

Purity is altogether difficult to achieve, and even harder to fake. O'Reilly's remorseful attempts at virtue collided with his catalogue of desires. I became his prey. Yet Melinda, my love, was also taken by him, thirty years her senior, none-the-less induced by his charm, his stoic, careful reactions, "Consecrate yourself, Melinda – purity." I should've been the priest! There are things we individually excel in, there are decisions that lead closer or further from our optimum vocation and suddenly – we are what we do and I Gypsy can't shake it.

Melinda loved cats. She would bring them in off the street, give them names like Ruth, Levi, Magdalena and then feed them Kittenkabuddle at the rectory until they couldn't walk. And always so willing to believe the best about a person, chatting away with the listless vagrants we fed at O'Reilly's soup kitchen every Saturday evening. I found myself competing for her attention and wondering how I could not win against even these stubble-faced urchins?

Did I mention that I have a history of heroin addiction?

Sweat bubbles on my forehead. The smell of creosote burns my nostrils. My ankle swells. Three bells chime faintly from St Louis Cathedral while a rat crawls overhead and stops. It slinks across a stringer and down the piling next to me. I kick my good leg but miss it and a rotten diagonal snaps.

"Come out and show yourself, I know you're down there." The dock cop's voice pitches low in the thick New Orleans air.

Show yourself, that's a strange choice of words. I never show myself. Not in a long while. It's against code. I uphold the code with blank stares; hide under hats, beards, long sleeves and aliases, my latest: Danny D'Agstino.

"Do you remember?" I had asked Melinda just after O'Reilly's knock and ill-fated encounter with a bullet, "the drive up the Hudson Valley in the Mustang with the top down and the heater blowing?" Her eyes suggested a navigation through a brain twing-twanged in opiates. "Do you remember the black-eyed Susans? We shared petals between our lips and you, laughing, trying to kiss me, sneezing with the flower powder smudged on your nose. We laid on the Indian blanket in the tall grass along the river. I plucked another flower and kissed you. You pulled up your skirt and whispered, 'Did you bring a condom?' I nodded and ripped open the Trojan and within seconds was engulfed in your heat."

84

Her eyes grew wide and she cantered, staring, crawling backwards with her arms and legs like a crab. She knocked the candle over. White wax gelled in the pool of blood that dripped from my side. And then she dropped. I pulled the needle from her arm and pushed her eyelids closed with my finger, the same finger that touched the dark knots, the contusions of Jesus.

"Show yourself. I know you're down there!" the dock cop yells again.

How many bullets would he fire? All you need is one – right through the heart. Kill all of me I pray, kill my soul especially, kill it first, if you can. The autopsy would show heroin; justified homicide, thieving junkie gypsy shot dead under New Orleans dock. And they would connect me with murder and other things in New York. The dock cop would be the hero, and I would be the corpse with all the clues. Even clues they would never know.

I hold tight to the piling now and watch the rat watching me. He's curious, this rat, wondering what kind of a merman I am, hanging under a dock in Ratville. I used to hang from a big limb on the oak tree and wonder when will I be like the rest of them? And Father O'Reilly with his curly hair would come by and watch us kids play and whistle with Uncle Frank, the mynah bird that sang like Prince. Sometimes O'Reilly would give us a ride in the white convertible and take us to the old rectory in the Bronx. And sometimes he would come only for me.

"You don't have to go. Stay home Yanko. Read your Shakespeare," my mother would say as she pushed her fingers through her cropped hair glancing at O'Reilly with his hand ready on the wheel. "Don't forget your heritage. We also have priesthood." I wanted to tell her everything, every detail, the dark, the rivers in his hand – a gypsy boy's story at 13. This authority he had, a foul authority and I, altar boy, sucked its vapor, chanting like Macbeth's witches, "fair is foul and foul is fair."

I told her more about the churning – the gypsy spirit. "It runs in the family," she offered. "Fortune tellers stand on our side of the river." I suspected the Romi strands inside me would never let go. Those odd moments in gypsy spirit struck me as real as the words across this page. I saw things, smelled things, tasted generational glimpses into the past like O'Reilly's mother sucking the breasts of a panting curvy domestic, the rosary dangling between areolas and a peach-fuzzed O'Reilly listening from across the hall.

Smack was good business. I paid Mother's grocers, her opera tickets, even her nouveau Manhattan rent. She asked once, "How long before you and the Catholic thugs are caught?"

I assured her I was merely dealing the deck and at the right moment I would challenge O'Reilly, at the highest level.

The dock cop calls into his radio. Blood runs down my arm to the elbow then drips into the Mississippi. The rat nibbles above and moves closer, its big ugly head moving up and down like O'Reilly at one of his goddamn celebrations. He would pass me sometimes in the hall of the cathedral and whisper, "The code of Christ," and his knotty hand would demure. "Listen to me now." And now, now, now would bounce around in my head.

Now, he loved her? I loved her first. I wanted to yell so everyone could hear: I LOVE MELINDA. They would turn their heads and look at the darkee who covets the white girl. I would give only the blank gypsy stare, while O'Reilly sucked from the chalice with one queer eye gazing at me in the mezzanine as I amplified the treble for his next act.

A plastic bottle spins in the gurgling whirl below me.

O'Reilly wore his collar that night. A healing he called it. "At the old rectory in the Bronx, Father?" It's Melinda's voice.

86

"Yes. We will pray for Thomas," O'Reilly's answer to everything.

Downriver, running lights move as if independent of each other, navigating the Big River's girth – green, red, and then only red. Now the ship's dark outline emerges, the stern swings out as it sets up for the bend at Algiers Point. I feel its power. It cuts through the thick night air, slicing the water, overpowering the current, phosphorescence in the foamy wake.

O'Reilly the rat moves closer with small movements of his hairy little legs. The dark hull of the ship passes. Tires click-click down the dock. They will find me.

The wake of the ship moves toward me. I hold tight, then drop into the river as the bulge of water surges off the bank.

I push hard into the current, cupping my hands, thrusting water. I ride the power of the ricocheted wake, propelling through the darkness of the Big River. My lungs ache. I want to suck air or water or her lips. Melinda's smooth pale face appears. Bubbles float up out of her mouth like round kisses. Her arms glide through the water – there's a yellow flower in her hair. O'Reilly, his hair chiseled like David, cuts in front of her, holding the drooping condom, his lips move, "Fornication, Thomas?"

Flow sweeps me downriver away from the light. I look back, throwing my head above the rips in the current. A faint blue flashes from a dock cop jeep, like the NYPD's lights that night as I staggered to the East River and hurled the pistol into its blackness.

The lights of the Ninth Ward twinkle in the distance. I'll catch duck water and float in like a corpse. Often I wish I was dead or never born – there is a difference, and now with this license I've been granted, by whom or what I hope to never know, I feel I may never die, stuck in a junkie's body, a gypsy soul able to see what priests cannot.

87

No, I'm normal! I'll stay in the current, down the Mississippi, into the sea and back up to New York in the Gulf Stream. A fresh start, a new chance – it didn't happen. I'm not a gypsy, I wear white clerics. I'll call Melinda.

But she doesn't have a number anymore. She doesn't have a yellow flower. She doesn't have eyes.

On the day we met she hugged me with her eyes, and I felt mercy for the first time. My love blossomed for her across the pews every Saturday afternoon, every Advent, every day became a Day of Passion. I was awkward, dumb, shy. I bought her things. "I was at Macy's and thought this would look, well, uh, exceptional around your neck," it might've been the first complete sentence I was able to demonstrate in her presence. "It's beautiful Thomas. Put it on me." Somehow I clasped the gold shackle with trembling hands. We were lovers now. I brought her many things; amulets, earrings, purses, chocolate and eventually, heroin.

The rip-rap is wired together with mesh. I pull myself up and into the soft wet grass of the levee. Down below, on the other side, the lights of the drawbridge flicker and 3AM traffic creeps along St. Claude Ave. I hobble across the iron, my footsteps making no sound. I feel the crimes of the bridge, the impaled cemented feet dropped here, and again here – a bridge of convenient death.

I don't know what happened that night at the old rectory in the Bronx, really. I too noticed the fast flush, the instant nausea. I stumbled to the East River, bleeding. It was hot, strangely hot for December in New York – I caught the A-train and made it to the Port Authority – a Greyhound south and settled in the seat watching the I-95 lights stream by feeling warm, wonderfully sentient as if all transgression had been lifted.

Somewhere en route to New Orleans, a woman appeared in the seat behind me. She leaned over and asked;

"Are you alright?"

"Completely."

She, by the grace of coincidence or gypsy luck or some other power, was a nurse. Her name: Melinda.

"You need a hospital," she said, examining my side with delicate fingers.

She spoke to the bus driver. He glanced in the huge rear view mirror, studying my slumped profile in the seat. She came back, I watched her as a tear oozed from her eye. She stroked my hair, squeezing me close to her bosom.

"Melinda? You've come back?"

The bus pulled over, an ambulance arrived. I remember this saint, holding my hand as they strapped me to a gurney.

After three days in the hospital, in the middle of the night, I slipped away, a tatterdemalion on journey. I'd always wanted to go to the Big Easy and had heard gypsies were at home there: paving driveways with cheap asphalt, collecting down payments on remodels that never happened. I walked the neutral grounds in a hot balmy reality, marveling at the scope of Jesus statues and the enormous density of wayward souls.

I lived on the lam, importing, and waiting for the moment. I was never quite sure what the moment held, but the gypsy sense informed me there was one to come. Then a fortune teller hailed me that night on Rampart Street on the edge of the Quarter as I walked from the Ninth Ward.

"Sit down," she said. "No, this chair." It was hers. "I've been waiting for you."

She asked, "What is your name?"

"Danny D'Agstino," I offered.

"No," she said, and reached across the table, grabbed the crucifix hanging from my neck, and jerked it off. "You are Yanko Grigori, priest of the Romi people." She held the crucifix out and touched the three points of the cross: "Rat, Elephant, Snake."

"Rat," I repeated slowly and a black one appeared at my feet. "Elephant," I continued and a monstrous one beckoned with its huge trunk at the door. "Snake," I said and the head of a coiled cobra rose from the table, its white fangs glittered as the split tongue quivered maliciously.

The palm reader bowed before me. I touched her on the forehead then turned and walked into the night, aware at last of my journey.

My shoes squish-squish across the oyster shells of the levee road. Heat from the early morning sun warms the back of my head. A mockingbird sings Prince from a telephone pole and the smell of coffee from the big roaster puffs by: puff, puff, puff. At Governor Nicholls Wharf, I punch in. The sun arcs above the red, yellow and blue warehouses. I climb up the gangway of the "Sucidava".

Sweat drips down my neck from under my hat while long sleeves cover my tracks. I watch the load of rubber swinging over my head across the deck and down onto the dock. The winch driver looks at me and shakes his head. He strips off his shirt. The Captain leans on the bulwark; I manage to smile, but he looks through me as if I didn't exist and turns away, his brow cocked as the final pallets of rubber lighten his ship. I look down at the river and a bloated dog bounces off the hull, spins in an eddy and floats away.

A man in black stands on deck his eyes sullen, his skin ashen white. I feel his crime – killer of spirit – monster, his eyes turn up in his head then light on me, the one who knows. I smell him. O'Reilly. Again and again.

In the corner of my eye I see the dock cops, their jeeps race down the wharf, tires clacking over loose dunnage. This is no routine patrol. It is my time, they've made the connection – was it the raft, the rubber, the finger prints? Did I leave a glove? The pistol in the East River?

I summon the spirit. The unfinished work. The derrick stops with a shriek, a clunk, mid cycle, vibrating in the deep bowels of the ship. Flames boil up out of the winch house. An explosion rocks the ship. Tendrils of orange heat ignite the black-garbed man in fire, his eyes caught in the horror of in-between-ness, the third place. "Welcome," I feel the tenor of those words pitch through my larynx.

The crew's feeble attempt to fight the fire is now abandoned as a great thrust of flesh runs to the railing, chunks of fire drop into the cargo hold and another explosion sucks away oxygen. I stand on the weather deck, the chronicler, a counter of death. The flames burn through me. I feel nothing. I am strangely manifest, full gypsy as I glide to the windlass. Wild men line the port gunwale jumping, the river waiting to catch their passion, their sin, their destiny. A rich community carbon floods my nostrils like a puff of myrrh and I am sitting with Father O'Reilly at the end of the unseen spiritual world, priest to priest, father to father, we're back in the booth, the lines in our palms like rivers, stretched, elongated, absorbing each other's sin.

Chef Menteur

My buddies call me Sing. The weather changes or somebody says "I'm going for a ride" and I start chanting "Ride, ride, ride, let it ride," or maybe a sign in front of a bar, "Tuesday's" and wham I'm singing "Stormy Monday but Tuesday's just as bad." Or like just the other day Noto was slapping Dell in the mouth with the ping-pong paddle and I start singing 'Joy to the World'. I don't know, it's weird, something to do with "the cognitive process," so says my shrink, Dr. Zsolt.

Dr Z. had the notion that I shouldn't have been there. Something about my Bristol-Myers score. He liked my tenor and said I was destined to become a great singer or something equally wonderful like an orthodontist. He never mentioned my lazy eye, my bony fingers, or that my left leg was shorter than the right. Once he suggested I should sell insurance when I got out because I displayed a "suffering countenance." All I had to do was stop believing all the bad stuff. "That's all there is to it," he'd say, "just think positive, think good things."

I liked Dr Z. but he seemed to be from a different planet, you know? Although he could surprise you like that Friday afternoon when he signed our weekend passes. He said our "team" had earned it, all five of us, even Noto. Weekdays are bad but weekends are even worse when you're stuck in the Good Holy Shepherd Christ Jesus Juvenile Detention Center. The place is a nut house. Steel bars everywhere you turn, blank walls except for the crosses, no windows and orderlies dressed in white telling you when to pee. Dr Z. was the only good guy there, but once I got out that door I had no intention of ever sitting in front of his desk again telling him what I thought about rivers that run dry.

Damon's porky little head barely topped the steering wheel. He was waiting for us out front in his mom's 1963 Ford Country Squire station wagon. It shimmered in the sun. Noto as usual, claimed shotgun. Panama and I stretched out in the back seat and Dell straddled the hump. The five of us decided to drive around and size up prospects. In the hot humid afternoon, prospects for action can be slim.

Scraps of breeze outside found their way to the back seat. It's good to have moving air in this kind of heat. Cools the sweat and chills the body. We stopped at a four-aisle store called Jo-Jo's. Damon parked in front by the pay phones and Panama went in for squares. Some cat with sunglasses and a radio pressed up to his ear danced in the shade of the store canopy, drinking from a brown paper bag. It sounded Motown. Couldn't catch the song.

Heat genies swirled off the Squire's hood. The cat with sunglasses put down his bag and now drummed on top of the Picayune machine; clang-clang cling, clang-clang, cling. Noto looked over his way and nodded; "Awright, where y'at."

Noto spoke charmer, also known as Yat. Some say it sounds more like Brooklyn than the South. He had it down, but I don't think he knew he had an accent. I don't think he'd ever been out of New Orleans. Thin, short, olive-skinned, full-lipped Italian with dark hair and big black eyes. He had an edgy pitch to his voice that sounded like an electric drill when he got excited. His mother worked for an escort service. Good lookin'. I'd seen her a few times in the Quarter.

"The guy say take anything you want! He quitting at midnight," Panama announced stepping out of Jo-Jo's with a carton of Coke, three quarts of ice cream and a hard pack of Marlboro balanced on top. Panama was a tall slender guy with a thin mustache. His father had been a Panama Canal pilot, but fell off the bridge of a ship while navigating through the locks and got chewed up by the prop. He told me his dad was drunk when it happened. His mother moved him to New Orleans hoping Panama would adjust. I hadn't known him long but I liked him. Maybe 'cause both our dads died drunk.

"I'm serious – he moving on. I no pay for this," Panama said from behind his load.

At once four doors opened on the Squire. I pulled up my jeans and walked in like I wanted to pay for something. The guy working had a big black mustache and a bald head. His left eye twitched and the muscles on that side of his face worked in concert pulling his mustache, his chin, his ear all into the same coveted point on his cheek. I thought he was sending me a signal.

"Go for the beer," Dell advised, peering through his thick lensed black-rimmed glasses.

I grabbed some Butterfingers, three cans of Vienna sausage and a handful of Bazooka. I curled my arm to make room for ice cream – Brown's Dairy. I started for the door then looked at the clerk. "Hey thanks man," I said walking out. He twitched. I dumped the stuff in the back seat and went back for more.

Noto marched up to Panama who was loading up a second time. "What are you doing with the toothpaste?" Noto cocked his head. "Think man – get the valuable stuff, cigarettes, shit like that."

"I need toothpaste. I get a brush for my momma too. A green one," Panama said.

Noto snarled then walked his load out. I looked over at Panama and studied his bright white teeth. "Hey, pick some toothpaste up for me too."

Noto came back – "That's it. Let's get out of here." The electric Yat had spoken.

94

Dell stumbled out with more beer. I could hear him thank the clerk but the clerk never said anything.

"Crank this fuck up. Let's go," Noto commanded.

Damon stepped on the gas and the Squire coughed, surged and almost cleared the hump at the entrance to Chef Menteur Boulevard. The tailpipe stayed behind.

Chef Menteur Boulevard is the main road that runs through east New Orleans. It's old Highway 90. If you stayed east it'll take you to Pensacola, go west, El Paso. It meant Big Liar, a French translation from the Choctaw who supposedly were disturbed by the tides that contradicted the flow of the bayou that now paralleled the boulevard. It was a subject of great interest to Dr Z. who told me the Choctaw meaning of the Big Liar was not as simple as it seemed. Occasionally he would lean across his desk and call me Chef Menteur.

Now the boulevard was littered with strip joints, burger joints, track homes, shrimp boats, boudin factories, a monstrous coffee plant and a rocket assembly plant – NASA. East New Orleans was where everything that didn't fit New Orleans went. Nobody chose to live there, it just happened.

"Who wants a Schlitz?" Dell yelled over the rumble of the Squire. He dug into the front pocket of his Levi's, pulled out a rabbit's foot with a church key and cut open a can then broke into his favorite chant, "Hell no. We won't go. Hell no. We won't go!"

"You'll go if you're looking at time. I'm going. I know I'm going," Noto said.

"What you talking about?" I asked.

"Don't you know anything, asshole? We're all going. Well, maybe not you." He laughed. "But the rest of us are. As soon as we turn 18 – first ship to Nam." He stared at me then turned away. "OK guys, keep cool. Drive to the shell road – let's see what we got."

95

Garbage gas from the dump mixed in the stiffening breeze as the tires of the Squire crunched along the shell road as we drove deeper into the marsh. The end of the road was our place. Nobody bothered us there. We parked by the shallow lake where a hundred years before loggers had cut the trees. Thousands of cypress stumps poked through the dark water like headstones in a cemetery.

Noto wanted all the stuff in the back of the Squire – inventory.

We opened the tailgate of the Squire and gathered outside, staring at our booty as dark clouds built up in the evening sky. Nobody said anything. I watched the ice cream melt trickling white goo onto the blue carpet. Finally I broke into song, "I love a parade, I love a parade, I love a parade – I dooo."

"Shut the fuck up," Noto interrupted. "OK, dig," he exhaled Marlboro smoke. "We're going to get down. Here's the plan – cash, straight up."

I ate my sausage thinking how Noto was so sure, barking out commands, never really caring what the others wanted, like my mother's second husband, the tall skinny Navy guy who wore a pea-coat. We had been driving through the outskirts of Baton Rouge late one night, the Navy guy driving. Mom and I sat in the back seat, his buddy rode shotgun. Mom begged them to stop. They were drunk and had a pistol. The thought of someone finding holes in the yield signs the next morning was too much for them to resist. My ears rang as the gun exploded again and again. We all got arrested that night. Well, I didn't exactly. I spent the night under the buzzing fluorescent light in the Sergeant's office. I wanted to tell the Sergeant, as he ate a bowl of red beans with a giant pickle, that it was a big mistake – I was a good boy, a perfectly good boy.

Noto's mouth: "Here's the deal; Damon you park around the corner, Panama you walk in first and start talking to your clerk friend. I'm going to stand at the door. Dell you stay in the car with Damon."

"So then what?" I asked.

"Then I want you to go the register and take the cash," Noto said.

"I hear the train a rolling, it's rolling round the bend, and I aint seen the... take the cash – why me?" I asked.

"I'll do it," Dell said.

"No, you won't. You're in the car remember? Sing's gonna do it 'cause Sing needs to get his hands dirty," Noto said.

"Alright," I said.

"Boogie," said Noto.

We drove back to Jo-Jo's. Damon cranked up the 8-track: Jefferson Airplane. Streetlights blurred as I stared out the window. There was this girl. Rebecca. We talked about traveling around the world together: Paris, Hong Kong, Tangiers. I kissed her once and she smiled and said I would make a good man someday. Then she and her family moved away. Ohio or someplace like that. "Don't you need somebody to loooove..."

We turned at Jo-Jo's.

"Cops," Damon said.

"See'm yeah. Drive down Chef," Noto said. "I got another idea."

"You're full of ideas tonight," I said as Damon accelerated.

"What about it?" Noto asked.

I didn't have it in me to take him on right then, besides, he had a knife. A six inch blade with a bone handle and a locking feature. Panama called it a "banana blade."

"They close at midnight, right?" Noto asked.

"Yes," said Damon.

"Still got that old 45?"

Dell farted and laughed. He was drunk now.

"Let this fucker off," Noto ordered.

"Hell no. I won't go," Dell said.

"Let him stay man. No problem," I said.

"No, he's out – get out. Pull the car over," Noto said.

Damon pulled over and stopped at the side of the Chef. There were no streetlights at this end of town, only the lights of NASA and the coffee factory. Dell didn't move. Noto stared at him, then me, then Dell again. He pulled out his knife. "Get the fuck out," he said, almost politely.

"Let him stay," I said.

Noto turned sharply. "I'll cut you up too."

"Take it easy man," Panama said slowly. "Isn't there any peace in this fucking world?"

Dell leaned, got his hand on the door handle and pushed. He eased over my legs and out, slow like as if daring Noto to stick him. He walked out into the night.

Damon punched it. Loose rock sprayed. We jumped the curb and drove down Chef Menteur. Nobody said anything. I studied Noto's scrawny neck. With one quick burst I could twist his head off. Or put a bullet in his brain. "Oh, give me a land where the buffalo roam and the deer and the antelope graze."

Noto turned in his seat and looked at me.

"So how's this gonna work?" I asked.

"You take the 45 and bust the locks off. Don't shoot'em off, pry'em off with the barrel. Like this." He worked the pistol like a crow bar with the barrel facing me. "There's two of 'em. I've seen 'em. They're weak. I don't think there's an alarm but if it trips, be cool – we got plenty of time. Panama and me are going in after you get the door down. Go for the valuable stuff, man – no fucking toothpaste! You're going to get anything in the cash register. Sometimes they leave rolls of quarters."

I listened as a semi passed us filling the motoring Squire with light.

"Damon, park in front. Lights out. Keep the motor running. Head for Chef Pass when we're back. Got it everybody?" Noto drilled.

"No, I don't got it everybody," I said.

"What's your problem Sing boy? Can't handle it? Maybe you want off like Dell?" Noto questioned.

"What makes you think you can give all the orders?" I asked.

"Listen, asshole. I know who I am, you don't." He laughed and stroked his hairless cheeks with the knife blade. Lightning flashed in the distance. Damon drove on.

Suddenly we were right there in front of Jo-Jo's. Before I knew it, I had the door down. It was easy, just like he said. We went in and I pulled the rolls of quarters out, just like he said. Noto plucked dried shrimp packets from a wall board and stuffed them in his pockets. Then a bell rang, loud, fast, metallic. I ran for the door and collided with Panama, spilling his take on the floor. Noto charged but slipped on a can and fell on his back. I stopped to help but it was too loud, I couldn't think. I ran for the door.

Outside I saw the Squire. The engine raced and through the windshield Damon's mouth gushed but I heard no words. I ran for the marsh. By the time I stopped I was deep in it, along the bank of the Big Liar – Chef Menteur. Green slime covered the bayou. An alligator slid in on the other side. I crawled away, through the thick grass into the woods. Then lights. From the boulevard. Beams shined all around me; cops or rabbit hunters?

I heard a shot and then a double pang, the kind of sound you hear when a bullet hits something soft. A wail – it sounded like Panama. They shot Panama!

I heard them pump load a shotgun. "Who's out there?!" one of them shouted. Their voices in discussion now, muted in the thick windy air. Lights sliced through the darkness again, toward the wail then toward me. I crawled. Back to the banks of Chef Menteur. Layers of mud oozed out from under me. I lost balance and fell, swallowing slime as I dropped below the surface. My foot hit something hard – a stump. I pushed against it and spun upwards moving my arms, cupping my hands thinking I would never make it to the other side, Dr Z. would never tell me the secret of Chef Menteur and I would sink instead into its dark waters.

I swam, quietly, through the green muck, to the other side. I crawled up the bank and lay there in the mud. The willow trees swayed and the commotion of their thin whips pitched high against a distant freight train's rumble. Steam from the coffee factory billowed, backlit by the glow of the plant. I got up and limped east toward the last traffic light in New Orleans. In the distance I could see it, it was late now, the light flashing yellow, swinging on the line. A storm was coming, but I couldn't sing.

Gyre

I reached out across the sheets and put my hand over the small of her back just above the skin, her camisole cinched, my mind in full focus as I encountered her aura. I breathed deeply thinking maybe this is the road back. It'd been awhile. I tried to think how long it'd been as I glided my hand above her butt feeling static generate from her panties, holding my hand just above contact like maybe the magic of silk and electromagnetism would change things.

In the beginning of our relationship she would turn to me late at night and ask questions like, "Do you think I have nice hands?" And words would slide out of my mouth, "slender, soft." She would listen and take it in and I could feel her smiling in the dark and we would make love.

We agreed, before we committed to each other, to live our relationship outside convention. The first step was not to get married. We made a list, Nina insisted, a list of everything we didn't want: the corporate world, jobs with time cards, doctors with pills.

It worked for a while. We lived in Pago Pago. Then, the problem of pregnancy, medical care – we moved to Hawaii.

"Do you think I have a nice penis?" I asked with my hand above the small of her back.

I waited for a giggle or even a sarcastic reply but she didn't say anything. I couldn't feel her smile; I couldn't feel her at all.

She rolled, caught my hand and pushed it aside.

Rent was due, jobs were tight and I was losing it. I lay in bed and listened to the dogs bark.

"A quickie would work," I offered.

She reached over and clicked on the light. Her big brown eyes took me in. "A quickie?" she asked. "I service you in lieu of who you are?"

"That's sarcasm, right?"

She gave me a gaunt look; trapezoidal lips that had nothing more to say. She clicked off the light.

"Maybe we should add it to our pact, no sex. Just so it's official," I said.

Our dining room table was square; wood, handsome except the chair pads were torn and released a dust of burnt-yellow foam. They bled synthetics like the plastic caught in the Pacific Gyre that swirls for years then washes ashore at Ka Lae; soy bottles from Korea, tiny yellow elephants from India, rope, bowling pins, fish nets, dolls, vodka bottles from Oregon. Synthetics were all over the house, in the bed, in the tub, on our feet.

We had drunk vodka tonics during the ocean film festival in Waimea. The alcohol added to the overall depression, films hissing truths – planet's going down faster than you think: rising CO_2 in the air, in the sea, global warming, climate refugees, and people carrying on like nothing's wrong.

We came home after a film on the vanishing bees and this fly started buzzing in the bedroom.

"Why did you let that fly in?" I had asked Nina, in a low flat voice.

"What fly?" she asked.

"That one," I pointed across the room.

"I didn't let the fly in."

"Flies disgust me. They carry pathogens, bacteria, germs. They displace bees."

She bolted for the door.

"Turn the light out," I shouted.

She threw a book at me then slammed the door.

Later that night I tried to coax her from her sleeping bag on the living room floor.

"I'm sorry," I said.

She rolled and faced the wall.

"I was testing a character profile," I said. "A guy named Malu, has a phobia for flies, reacts to a late night buzz in his bedroom."

She rolled over, "Asshole."

"Did you hit me with Jack London or *Beaches of the Big Island*?"

"Look Sergei, we're out of balance," she had said.

Between the barks I heard rain. A cow mooed in the distance.

Maybe we're just incompatible, I thought, like our chemistry oxidized with the vog, the volcanic ash spewing out of this island, or maybe the stress of no work and endangered big eye tuna and global warming and everything – on the verge of collapse, we're all feeling the power of this thing – Aleuts, Bangladeshis, Pacific Islanders, climate refugees by the millions – we're in the end game, the earth is going down and this mounting pressure has fractured Nina's super-sensitivity to the planet and caused her to become frigid.

There, I thought, practical male sniffs out problem: environmental stress, stresses relationship. I exposed the mechanics. At the same time I recognized a pattern in the way I think – contexts nested in my mind, presuppositions that guaranteed a certain result, like pads for comfort. I nudged up against this truth, this gyre, but I couldn't swim out of it.

The rain pattered against the roof. I wanted to unravel.

Nina cleared her throat. "I just want you to know," she said. "I can't go on like this."

"Neither can I," I interrupted. There was a worm in my abruptness but I couldn't process it. I sputtered and offered, "I'm applying at the restaurants tomorrow."

"Sergei," she said. My name hung in the dead space of the room; no barking, no mooing. The rain had stopped. She stared at me in the dark. I was caught in my name, who I was, who I am.

The phone rang.

"Captain Stig?"

Nina clicked on the light. The kids woke.

"Two thousand a month straight-time?" I asked. "Factory trawler, South China Sea, the Pacific Integrity."

I put my hand over the phone and whispered. "I can send at least eighteen hundred back."

Nina watched me.

"Today?" I asked.

"Hilo, Honolulu, Taipei, Kaohsiung," I repeated.

I looked at Nina. Her big brown eyes had nothing to say and at that moment I remembered it was Valentine's Day almost a year ago since we last made love and then I realized, we would never do it again.

Six Head

Harper, Texas is not everybody's choice for a weekend destination. But my new boss, head purveyor of Lister's Bowinkle Ranch, a giant spread among spreads, was short-handed and needed six head delivered to Raz's Livestock Auction. I'm not a cowboy, I'm a bookkeeper, but it was cowboy work – so I put on my boots the next day, logged the mileage and left at 6AM climbing Forty Mile Hill with 3 tons of hoof attached wondering if I should listen to country and western. I pushed in a CD of Iggy Pop instead.

Low clouds burned off in the distance, but then high in the sky I noticed a parallelogram cloud. Symbolic for sure, I thought. Something was up.

Six hours later I rolled into Harper. A giant Texas flag fluttered above a Chevron and three men in camo-jackets smoked beneath it eyeing two buffalo, whose gutted, still-steaming remains covered the deck of a thirty foot flatbed.

I kept driving, slowly, down Highway 90, looking for Raz's. In the distance pick-ups of all styles lined the road; step sides, dualies and long beds. Stetsoned heads shuffled along the shoulder. A black metal hog with red painted eyes caught my eye. Welded to a gate the sign warned: "No Bears, Cats, Wolves or Coyotes – NO CAMERAS."

I stopped at the ticket booth and asked the lady where she wanted the cows.

"Cows?" she questioned. Her turquoise glittered in the sun.

"Miniature Herefords."

She took a good look at me. "Take your minis down to the back shoot, darling."

I backed in the trailer without killing anybody.

"Whatcha got there?" the chute man asked.

"Six head," I said, wishing I had worn a cowboy hat.

"Head of what?"

"Cows. Minis."

"Sex?" he asked.

I shook my head.

"Jeremy get in there and see what the man brought us."

Jeremy opened the trailer gate and checked the cargo. "Heifers," he called out, looking at me.

A high pitched shriek pierced the air.

"What's that?" I asked.

"Black Buck – don't like pens," the chute man said, nodding toward the corrals.

I looked over the top of the railing. About twenty animals three foot tall with spiraled dark horns, and elf-like faces paced in a pen. One shrieked, jumped into the wood, bounced off and fell on its cousins. In the next pen two water buffalo with big sad eyes and short thick horns looked up. Next to them, a Zebra. I looked down the row of iron: Reindeer, Axis Deer, Impalas, Buffalo, Multan Sheep, Aoudad, and Shetland Ponies.

"Had a giraffe in here once," the chute man said. "Couldn't get him under the roof – had to auction'em off outside."

Jeremy handed me the papers. I said, "Much obliged." He spat brown juice and said, "Good Luck."

I walked past the fowl department. Live chukars, quail, pheasant, and peacocks were boxed up with number tags wired to their cage.

"Interested in any bird action today?" the bird man asked.

I spread my own wings and banked around the corner.

A man with a monkey on his back stood at the front door of the auction auditorium. The primate's tailed curled around monkey man's crotch.

"Wanna buy her?" he asked, lifting an eyebrow. "Golden Squirrel Monkey, Congo, pleasant animal. Believe she might cotton to you." He winked then smiled revealing several teeth.

"Not today, thank-you." I walked into the auction house.

Bleachers in a semi-circle surrounded a white painted iron bar cage. Inside the cage, doors on both sides seemed proportioned for elephants. Elk horn chandeliers spread across the ceiling like webs spun by nervous spiders. Lights flickered. Two burly dudes appeared at the doors in Army jackets with big sticks. The auctioneer stood tuxedoed above us in a red-lit platform suspended in the air by a crane. He tapped the podium with a conductor's wand, cleared his throat and after explaining the rules offered everybody a happy Sunday.

The door to the right swung open and a high-stepping Black Buck jumped to center stage. It lowered its head, circled once, looked up and sniffed. Then it tapped the dirt floor with a paw, let out a shriek, and leaped across the stage whacking his horns against the white metal bars.

"Hey now, hey hey give me five, give me five, give me five huuuundred," the auctioneer bantered. He recited the chorus several times then stopped. He looked out; gimme hats, camo jackets and facial hair. The men dressed that way too.

"This is a fine specimen," the auctioneer noted in a soft sympathetic voice. "Now who's gonna give me five hundred dollars to start this thing off?"

A hand with five fingers rose in front of me.

One of the door dudes popped the Black Buck and it jumped twenty feet.

Beer Breath leaned over and said: "Them blacks can jump."

"I got five now give me five and a half. Five now five now give me five and a half."

The man in front of me bought the Black Buck for 650 dollars.

A portly man in a leather vest and a bolo tie next to me nodded, leaned in.

"That feller runs a huntin' ranch down the road. Takes orders from Dallas and Houston. Comes here, buys'em and sets'em loose. They drive down and shoot'em, like they've done something," he said, shaking his head, like fair play had been breached for the first time in the Lone Star State.

I walked out to the concession stand.

"Do you carry any vegan products, perhaps a meatless taco?" I asked.

The girl's eyes rolled.

"You're funny," she said.

I rambled past a rusting 57 Chevy on jacks then out through the gate. I opened the door to the truck and Iggy Pop fell out. I picked it up, plugged it in then checked the sky for parallelograms.

Dear Oswaldo

I've never known a fat barber. They're usually skinny, trim. Makes you wonder how they keep fit. Like they have a double life. I was pretty sure this Dominican barber had a double life. I bet my career on it.

I'm sure you're not fat. Although if you are it's OK. I never gave much thought to being a barber. I guess you did, during your formative years. I'm sorry I wasn't there much. I might have steered you in another direction. Probably that barber your mother married, Henry Home-at-Six. They still together, still in Miami Shores?

I've been married four times. I don't know if you know that. It's the national average for cops. Looking back at it, your mother was, by far, the best. I'm a bit of a fool. Mistakes, I'm learning, are part of it, part of life. But at some point you've got to get clear. And I was pretty clear about this Dominican barber.

I'd had him under surveillance; he flew to Miami once a month, stayed for a day or two, sometimes a week. Drove a Dodge, hung out at a Brazilian restaurant called Ipanema. Slept in an apartment near the river, where they load ships for the islands. I staked him from under a banyan tree in a ghost. I watched him pull something out of a black bag. Polished it. Sounds like a small detail but everything matters. Tools of the trade, no doubt, probably a scalpel. This guy wasn't everything he appeared to be – not just a barber.

I thought about you that night under the banyan tree. Maybe it was the country and western or maybe it was the scotch. I don't know. I don't know if you married or if you have kids or if you go home to Jupiter at night and just watch ESPN. It's OK, I'm in no position to judge.

I spent 23 years on the force. Often I just wanted to go home and watch TV myself, but the business is demanding. Crooks don't sleep. They breed like dogs. And they're failing less and less.

Last year Dade approved a new policy; the international plan. If you got seniority like myself, you don't need a 331 – permission. You just go. Use your own judgment. If there's a snitch in the department and sometimes there is, it eliminates that variable. So it's not the first time I went south on my own.

I had to arrest this guy in his own country, undercover, tricky. Handcuff him, I thought, fit him with the bracelet, get his files and hope he comes clean.

I sat in his chair. That's what you call it I think, a chair, a station, at a barber shop across the street from Parque Central. He comes on like a pro, neat, you know, perfect hair, platinum glasses, trimmed mustache, white guayabera. His station is in the corner near the back door. I tell him what I want. He looks at my hair, my beard and says OK. Then he gets the scissors out and I'm thinking if he makes me, slit, right through my jugular and boom! he's out the back door.

Turns out he cut my hair real well.

I'm watching him for signs through the mirror; twitches, blinks, quirks. He wants to take my glasses off but I insist. I don't know if you wear glasses, but it's hell when you have to take'em off. Keep that in mind for your next customer.

He's shaving my beard – you know the name of that tool, I don't. It's got a low buzz, tickled my Adam's apple. Somebody out front lays on the horn and I think if I make a mistake, if this is not Raul Garcia, the surgeon – El Cortero, the one that works over all the top drug pins in Colombia, I'm through in Dade, maybe everywhere.

Garcia is a master at changing profiles. He's not just a surgeon; he's an artist: noses like Kardashian, ears like Assad. The biggest difference can be the eyes, not the color; you can do that with contacts, but the shape. You shoulda seen the before and after of Lazlo Martinez. Took the Hungarian right out of him.

The lieutenant thought I might be barking up the wrong tree. I'd had a string of those. I needed a bust to show I wasn't washed up. A comeback. Last year I thought I had the Liberty City Kid, turned out to be just a kid from Liberty City. Then there was that barber in Homestead. I was sure he was fronting for the Diablos. The lieutenant warned me, we go way back, but I knew, blowing this Dominican deal could be my last. I felt the pressure, had a little trouble myself sitting in that chair without twitching.

Outside – traffic, motorcycles everywhere, two-stroke, loud, blowing blue smoke. Then there's the music. Biggest goddam speakers I've ever seen – in the cars, on the sidewalks, the balconies. They say the Dominican Republic is the loudest country in the world, after India.

He asked me, "Bastante?"

I said, "No. Corte un poco mas, estile Dominicano." I pulled at the hair hanging over my ears.

He looked at me and nodded. Takes out the scissors again.

So how's your mother?

She still wear that turquoise headband? Is she fat now? Tell me she is. It'd make me feel better. God I hope she's 500 pounds. No I don't. I really don't.

What can I say? Twenty years since I last saw you? You have the right, sorry, sounds like Miranda. I wouldn't blame you if you didn't read this. It's OK. But I want you to know that I do care for you. I had my priorities wrong; detective first, husband, father a distant second, way distant. In many ways you must be like me. DNA. Use it all the time in forensics. Do you wake up some mornings and think whatever you do will fail?

So the Dominican barber takes the cloth away, brushes me off and presents me with a bill for 200 pesos. Not bad, I think, five bucks for a shave and a haircut. Then I punch him in the head with the brass knuckles. He buckles. I pull him out the back door and handcuff him to the seatbelt in the back seat of the rent-a-car.

I burn rubber driving out. Brake hard thirty feet later. A dump truck stops and blocks both lanes. I try to back up, but I'm pinned by a zillion motorcycles. A kid starts to wash my windshield. I say no but he keeps washing. I see the lady from the front desk and some of the other barbers running down the sidewalk.

The dump truck driver jumps out. He looks at me then waltzes to a coffee stand. A cop shows up and I think he wants to know why I didn't pay the window washer. He looks in the backseat. "Boracho," I say, he's drunk. The cop sees the handcuffs. I pull out my badge. Long story short, I spent nineteen days in a Santiago jail. Dade finally bailed me out. Turned out the guy was just another skinny barber. I got early retirement.

The sun's up this morning. That helps. Wasn't sure if I should write this. Whether you would read it or care, or if it matters. It does matter. Everything matters. By the way, I quit drinking. I go to meetings and I'm working on a comeback. I'm taking a chance this letter won't fail.

Swords Hanging on the Wall

"My father, Franz Josef Schennach, was a gendarme, Hauptmann, in Tirol. After the Nazi took over, he had to prove that he was Aryan. He could not prove this," Anna Stenson said. She looked across the room from her chair.

"Brown eyes go to Africa... They taunted me. At school. Only the blue eyes would stay in Europe, if Hitler won. I was hoping he would not," she said adjusting the hem of her skirt.

Doctor Gross rubbed his mustache as he sat at his desk under the ceiling fan that cut the air with a clickety-click, clickety-click.

"You do not speak much, do you?" she asked, pausing, her lips tight as a hint of a breeze outside stirred the leaves of the trees.

"The smell in here is also strange.

"And by the way, yesterday, I turned 44. For your information."

She watched a beetle buzz through the open window. "So many flying things?"

Then her eyes opened big. "I told Altmann, he came to my birthday party of course, I told him about a man at my father's funeral who was dressed in black. Baggy black coat, black hat. This man reached into the deep pockets of that coat and gave me coin. It was 1939. I was five.

"Now I know his name was Isidor Schennach. I often asked my mother who he was. She never answered, changed the subject and said don't ask so many questions. Someone at the funeral told me to call him Uncle Isidor." Anna Stenson rubbed the bridge of her nose.

"Papa used to sit me on his knee und bounce me – humpaaa humpaaa rider, humpa humpa," She smiled then her face turned solemn. "He disappeared after work one day. A few weeks later, Mama get a postcard from him, saying he was on a train, on his way East, did not know where to, said he would ask someone to mail the card.

"Later he was at the railroad station in Buchers on the Moldau, in the Czechland enroute to Poland, and I noticed this only recently, but his title on a picture was no longer Hauptmann, but Hauptwachmeister. They were sending him to Majdanek to be a guard?

"And today I typed in Isidor's name and found he died at the concentration camp in Dachau. Prisoner No. 43651. Altmann had asked me a question and that is why I looked."

She pushed back against the chair.

"I do not like the air in here.

"The odor is not correct.

"When will you talk?

"Ja. Well. Then I will finish the story, since I started it.

"Papa died in Buchers. Pneumonia, they said. His body, or I should say his coffin, was sent back on the train to our home in Tirol, but I never saw his body.

"I grew up thinking every tall man in uniform was Papa.

"There. I am finished talking. I really don't know why I am here. I was shocked what I had found out today. I am asking you. Why am I here? Since you are the source you must tell me," she said.

"Source?" Doctor Gross asked.

"Yes. You seemed to have arranged this meeting, if that is what it is," she said, pushing her black hair back. "If you think that I am not in charge of my faculties, then you are sorely mistaken."

She looked at the ceiling. "Who else is here?"

"Millions," Doctor Gross said. His eyes glanced at the office door then across the courtyard to the iron gate where the arch above read, 'Tribunal Düsseldorf'. "Millions came through the gates but only a few have come through that one – justice."

Dr. Gross lifted his head as he took in a deep breath and held his pointy chin parallel with the floor for a long second, then he picked up the tongs and dropped an ice cube into his glass.

"Is Uncle Isidor here?" she asked, looking intently at the doctor.

"Materially?" he asked.

"Yes materially? What kind of question is this you give me?"

"Is he wearing a baggy black coat?" the doctor asked.

"Yes."

"He could be here then."

"Is Papa?"

"Why not."

"Papa! Oh – oh my God. Mein Gott. Mein Gott." Anna Stenson clasped her hands to her face.

"What is he wearing?"

"He is in uniform."

"Oh! Papa! Papa is here. Papa is here! Papa is home! May I see him? Please may I see him?"

"Momentarily, I ..."

"Is Mama here?"

"No."

"But why not?"

"She is not here."

"She, but, but, thank-you. Thank-you for talking to me.

"I would like to see Papa now, Doctor Gross."

"Who sent him to Poland?"

"The Nazis of course."

"Yes, but who in particular? Someone must've signed the order from your town."

"Hans Leitner. He was the head Nazi in Jennbach. Momma told us to be very careful with him. Lived on the top floor. They threw the others out. We had part of the second. My best friend was Katia, his daughter. They had many swords hanging on the wall," she said.

"Hans Leitner," he said, writing on a tablet. "What did you feel about this man Leitner sending your father away?"

"I did not know about those thing then. And nobody helped me to figure them out. Mama and everybody kept their lips zipped." She brought her thumb and index finger and moved them across her lips. "Am I criminal for not knowing?"

"Criminal?" Dr. Gross asked.

"Yes. We who survived. We did not feel the pain. The fullness. To be so close and survive. Somehow this must be criminal."

"Your memory is improving Ms. Stenson," Dr. Gross said, looking at the clock. "I will see you next Thursday, same time."

"Suddenly you have taken interest," she quipped. She lifted her nose and sniffed. "It's the bomb shelter smell. How did you capture it?"

Dr. Gross took a sip of his drink then moved his eyes up at the ceiling fan, clickety-click, clickety-click.

Hot Water

In the shower she sat on the ledge, naked, the water splashing off the tiles.

"It won't get hot," she said, looking up. Her legs stretched diagonally across the shower floor.

The man looked at her, down at her legs covering the tiles, the water splashing, the razor in her hand. He put his hand to the water at the shower head.

She reached and pulled the razor slowly up her calf. "What was the man's name that wrote about those killings? Just down the road. In Holcomb. Did you realize that? Ten miles away. They killed that family in cold blood. Who wrote that book?"

"I don't know. Who was it?" he asked, shaking his hand free of water.

"I'm asking you."

The man glanced at the vanity mirror then down at her. "Let's see." He lifted his head. "Philip Seymour Hoffman played him in the movie."

"Right," she said. "Marvelous. Wasn't he marvelous? What's he done lately?"

"Nothing I suspect. He's dead," the man said.

"Dead?" she asked and rolled her hips to shave the other leg.

"OD'd on heroin. That's all I know."

"Heroin?"

"Better than sex, I heard," he said.

The spray splashed between her legs.

"The water is still not getting hot," she said. "Look, goosebumps." She held an arm up.

"I must've hooked up the tank wrong. I'm sorry. I'll check it later. At least it's kinda warm." Outside the Kansas sun beat against the bathroom window.

"Goosebumps are a sign of chills. Did you know that?" she asked.

"I bet that family down the road had the chills."

She laid in the shower with the small of her back against the ledge, her legs spread, moving the razor now carefully along her vagina. "Don't you remember his name? He was from the south, Alabama, I think. Raised by women."

"I know who you're talking about. I can't quite bring it up." He felt a bulge in his pants as he looked down at her, trimming.

"In Cold Blood – that was the title," she said.

"He was alcoholic. Homosexual," he said.

"And a genius," she said. "This razor is dull. What if I used your old-fashioned thing?"

"I'll get it for you."

He turned to the medicine cabinet and looked again into the mirror then pulled out the razor. He handed it to her.

She twirled the metal handle between her fingers then pulled it across her skin, "Ouch," she said. Blood trickled along the inside of her thigh, diluting as it streamed through the drops of shower water.

"I'll lick it off," he offered.

"No. I just have to be careful," she said. "I wish I could remember his name."

"Me too. It seems like life is hinging on this guy's name," he said.

"No life goes on."

"Not really. We have about thirty years left. The species, I mean, global warming, food shortages and all."

"That's depressing," she said.

"It's fact," he said.

"I wonder if Philip Seymour Hoffman knew that." She looked up and studied the man's face. "You could use a shave yourself."

"Would you shave me?"

"I would but you're so practical – got all these nice depressing answers."

"I just want a shave with that blade. And I want you to do it. Naked."

"I'm going to leave my pussy half-shaved. Don't you think it looks nice that way?" She arched her torso, exposing light brown on one side and skin and stubble on the other with a bubble of blood.

"No. I don't. You should shave it all."

"I'll shave you but only one side of your face – would you like that?"

"I wouldn't. When you shave it should be complete."

"Complete? You can't even think of that man's name?"

"Recall dysfunction."

"Another practical answer. The species is dying off and you're still clinging to nice neat answers."

"When we're gone we'll just be a nice neat layer of soil."

"That's right. A layer of soil." She stood up in the shower and washed off the clipped hairs and the blood.

"It won't really mean anything," he said.

"Of course it will. The murder of that family has meaning."

"Meaning? Maybe, but later it won't mean anything."

"I'm half-shaved and you're half-baked." She turned the water off. "Hand me a towel please. Do I have to tell you everything?"

"Like we were never here," he said, pulling a towel from a shelf.

"But we are here."

"Who's to know?"

"Whatever being follows us, that's who."

"Not sure if intellect will make the cut." He dropped the towel on her back.

"You can't remember that man's name and now you're telling me we're just a spoof in the universe," she said, bent-over, toweling a leg.

"Spoof?"

"If there's no meaning we might as well be spoofs," she said.

"Spoof of what?" he asked.

"Spoof of civilization."

"Or the civilization that was a spoof," he said.

She stood up with the towel wrapped around her body. "You've already suggested that."

"Why is his name so important?"

"Because he's no spoof. He actually did something."

"He told a good story."

"Yes. Stories matter. Murder matters. Meaning matters," she said. "Why am I with you?"

He looked in the mirror again and followed the contour of his nose with his finger. "Penis size?"

"Penis, all hail the penis. If it received no attention, what would you do? Have a meaningless life?"

She sat on the commode. He listened to her urine spray against the porcelain of the toilet.

"You should go." She shook her wrist beckoning toward the door.

They looked at each other, then he lifted his eyes toward the shower head. "Tomorrow I'll fix the hot water."

"No, I'll call a plumber," she said.

"The men who killed that family were plumbers," he said.

She stared at him. He took several steps then stopped at the bathroom door, turned and said, "Truman Capote."

Ninety-six Dollars

Jim stood in the kitchen heating the spoon over the flame of the stove while he thought about the old man in his jacket in the July sun taking small steps from his house to the garage to check on the progress. He could not remember the color of the old man's eyes. They were not blue, he was sure of that.

Jim tapped the rig. A bubble floated up and he tied off. The teenagers were at Grandma's and his wife was out with the baby. Cool air blew from the wall registers, but to Jim it seemed hot. It had been hot all summer.

The old man's name was Mansel. Jim had been arrested by a sheriff named Mansel in Louisiana, but the old man wasn't a sheriff. He had asked Mr. Mansel if he was from Louisiana. Mr. Mansel had said, no, he was not from there.

"You can have those shears if you want, I won't be needing 'em," Mr. Mansel had said.

Mr. Mansel hired him to clean out his garage. There were lots of things the old man didn't want; jars of screws, hinges, a couple of hoses, herbicide, fertilizer, boxes and boxes of fertilizer: pellets in green boxes and cones in white boxes. You placed the cones in a hollow steel tube and ran a hose through it to inject fertilizer. Jim had never seen one before.

A rope had hung from a rafter in Mr. Mansel's garage. Jim saw himself swinging on it, the noose tight around his neck, his body swaying freely back and forth and then he was at a dairy farm in a barn with rows of mooing cows attached to machines and the smell of milk and cow shit and he hovered over his own naked cadaver and Mr. Mansel walked in, looked up and walked out.

An axe with a red handle had leaned in the corner. "You can have that too," Mr. Mansel said. "My grandson doesn't want it." Mr. Mansel looked away, out toward the bluffs.

Jim had asked Mr. Mansel about the weather in the valley.

"Lightning," he had nodded toward the charred top of a mountain. Then he turned and walked back to his house.

The phone rang, but Jim did not move. He was sick. It happened every time.

In a perfect world he could shoot up and not feel that dizzy, helpless free fall. Vomit-on-the-wing, he called it. In that world everybody would be on heroin.

The box of linoleum tile, green and black, that Mr. Mansel had given him, was still stacked on the kitchen floor. His wife had nixed it. Jim had also kept the rope and the axe and at the last minute he kept the fertilizer too, putting it in the keep pile. He had put the jars of screws and hinges in the throw away pile.

Mr. Mansel had come out again while deer were chomping on corn pellets in the backyard. "I've been feeding them for thirty years," Mr. Mansel said. He didn't address Jim, he had just said it, like a general comment about the passage of time and the habits of deer.

Jim had picked up a box of rat poison and a package of D-Con Roach Killer with a faded picture of Mohammed Ali on the label. Mr. Mansel had looked at the poison and then said, "I need you to sweep over there." He pointed.

Mr. Mansel had been a principal at schools throughout Texas and then had taught in the education department at the university. "I taught all levels," Mr. Mansel had said, and that's all he said about it, as if it were a big waste of time, leading people out of ignorance.

Jim rolled off the couch and pulled his pants on. He left his shirt off and then he looked in the mirror. She'll never know he thought to himself. He looked at his chin, then his nose, then his eyes. Jim's washed-out face hung on his neck like a cheap cotton baby doll. His clammy hands drooped along his side as he swayed outside and stashed his shit in the false bottom of the rocker panel on his truck.

He picked up the weekly newspaper, opened it and set it on the table like he was reading it. The tabby slunk by, meowed and rubbed against his leg.

At the end of the afternoon with the floor swept and the two piles of stuff stacked in the truck, Mr. Mansel had come out again and looked over the garage.

A blue flashlight lay on the counter. "You can have that too. I won't be needing it."

Then Mr. Mansel asked, "How much?"

Jim added some numbers on a brown paper bag then held it out. "Ninety-six dollars."

Mr. Mansel did not take the brown paper. He only repeated the number as if ninety-six was a significant amount, not in its value of labor but in the number itself, as if ninety-six was the number of the day or the week or the most significant number in his life. Ninety-six hung in the air and you could feel Mansel absorbed in it. He repeated the number. "Ninety-six." It slid out of his mouth like it was the clearest thing ever stated. And then he looked down at the clean swept floor and said quietly, "Ninety-six dollars."

Jim had used part of the money to buy a dime bag. Mexican H. Nobody will know, not even the P.O. There was that shit you could buy, take it right out of the system, he thought.

A car drove up the driveway and Jim heard the baby crying and then he looked down at the newspaper and saw the obituary of Russell Royce Mansel. He bit down on his tongue. He couldn't feel a thing.

Luck

Lori got swept out to sea about two hours ago. Yes. Sure did. Playa Grande. I saw her in the zone, then checked again, beyond the breakers. She waved. She waved again. Fuck. I handed my glasses to Mesa and Reef and yelled Stay on the beach. I ran. Heart pumping crazy. Hit the surf. Swam. Big MFer comes. Under or over? Over. Wrong. Swim through another, under this time, and another and another. Where is she? I'm fuckin' dying. There. I spot her. Blurred. I get there. Somehow. She's scared. I'm scared. I'm glad you're here, she says. I'm spent. The waves are breaking. Big. Gotta get back. Hold on I say, hold on to my waist. I'm swimming hard with what I got left. Not much. We surf one, we surf another but this one sucks us down. And out. GD, I think this is it. Something in my mind clicks, swim diagonal. Diagonal. Then a rock. A fucking rock in the sea. Five seconds on a lucky rock. Recharge. Mouth just above the froth. Next wave knocks us down. It's enough. We surf another and gain. I see the beach, the final line of breakers. Crashing. Touch. Sand. Mesa at the shoreline. Reef building castles. Friday the 13th. Luck.

About the Author

Richard Mark Glover has had short stories published in *Oyster Boy Review*, *Bookend Review* (Best of 2014), *Crack the Spine*, *Buffalo Almanac*, and won the 2004 Eugene Walters Short Story Award, for *Chef Menteur*. His journalism has appeared in the *San Antonio Express News*, *Ke Ola* and the *Big Bend Sentinel* where he won the 2010 Texas Press Association Best Feature Award, medium size weekly, for *Just Another Night in Marfa*.

Previously Published

Chef Menteur (*Oracle*, Winter 2004, Winner Eugene Walters
        Short Story Award 2004)
Hillbilly Armor (*Oyster Boy Review*, Winter 2010)
Birds (*Sinister Tales*, Fall 2009)
A New Country (*Dogplotz*, Spring 2008)
Window Cleaner (*Weird Year*, 2011)
Clausen's Farm (*Canary*, Spring 2011)
Dear Oswaldo (originally published as 'Dear Gerald',
        Twisted Dreams Magazine, April 2014)
Our Lady (*Kentucky Review,* Jan 2016)
        (Originally published as 'The Gringa', an audio
        recording for *4'33" Magazine*, London, Summer 2013)
Further Than It Looks (*Rope and Wire*, December 2013)
Ninety-Six Dollars (*Static Movement*, 2009)
Foucault Hill (*Buffalo Almanac*, March 2014)
Luck (*First Stop Fiction*, March 2014)
Gyre (originally published as 'Synthetics', *Book End Review*,
        Best of 2014)
Do You Think I Talk Funny? (*Crack the Spine*, March 2014)
Six Head (*Pure Slush*, July 2014)
Nothing Really Ordinary (*Jelly Fish Review*, 2015)
Product, (*Kzine* Issue 15, 2016)
Dark Energy with Its Foot on the Gas (*Five Pure Slush Vol. 10*,
        Pure Slush Books, January 2016)

Swords Hanging on the Wall (*Literally Stories*, Apr 2016)
Hot Water (*Orthogonal*, 2016)
Human Potential (*Corvus Review*, 2016)

Also from Truth Serum Press

http://truthserumpress.net/catalogue/

The Miracle of Small Things

978-1-925101-73-7 (paperback)
978-1-925101-74-4 (eBook)

The Miracle of Small Things beguiles the reader with a witty and compassionate portrait of a year in the life of Luis Villalobos in tropical Curaçao, where nothing is quite what it seems, and all can be lost or gained in a summer afternoon on the beach. Told deftly, with humor and insight into our very human vulnerabilities, this lovely novella by Guilie Castillo Oriard builds upon that quest for happiness we share, a sense of belonging, and makes me want to travel south to find my own miracle.

Also from Truth Serum Press

http://truthserumpress.net/catalogue/

Based on True Stories

978-1-925101-75-1 (paperback)
978-1-925101-76-8 (eBook)

The small fictions in *Based on True Stories* will not lull you – they will piss you off or, at the least, move you to indignation, or tears, or laughter. Maybe all three. These gems provoke, like the tip of a chef's knife pricking skin, and just as the words get uncomfortable, the story delivers the bit of redemption that reveals the humanity of his characters – and of us all. These stories are real, raw, and honest. The reading doesn't get much better than that.

Also from Truth Serum Press

http://truthserumpress.net/catalogue/

happyme@t.us

978-1-925536-07-2 (paperback)
978-1-925536-08-9 (eBook)

To be everywhere and nowhere, all at once ... Through her stories, Kim Conklin takes us on a journey of the human condition, where the everyday becomes foreign and dangerous, while the oddities of our world provide us with strange comfort. Each story is unsettling, passionate, thoughtful, provocative and reaffirming; taking the reader everywhere and nowhere, all at once. Dark tales, deftly told.

Also from Truth Serum Press

http://truthserumpress.net/catalogue/

Rain Check

978-1-925536-09-6 (paperback)
978-1-925536-10-2 (eBook)

Beautifully rendered, the stories in *Rain Check* could well be the footprints and photographs of our own lives if we'd have taken risks as daring as Noe's characters. Each misstep, triumph and regret rings true. Reading these stories is like being a lucky voyeur who happens upon an artist with brush in hand, nearing the finishing touch of their masterpiece. Nothing is more potent than prose that lifts off the page and lands, like a well-placed bullet or caress, on the heart, and that's precisely what Noe has done here.

Also from Truth Serum Press

http://truthserumpress.net/catalogue/

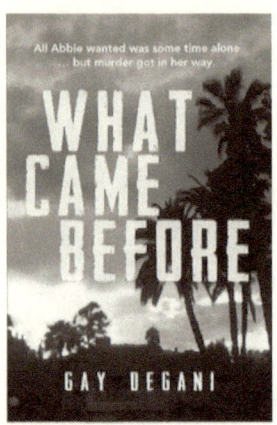

What Came Before

978-1-925536-05-8 (paperback)
978-1-925536-06-5 (eBook)

Five words scribbled on a discarded piece of paper ignite old memories for Abbie Palmer and leads to the explosive uncovering of a fifty-year-old mystery. *What Came Before*, Gay Degani's debut novel rumbles along at break-neck speed. I've long enjoyed the quirky characters and tightly-written plots of Ms. Degani's short stories and her novel didn't disappoint me. The book presents great characters, including a strong older-female protagonist, and ably-managed twists and turns through the streets and people of modern-day Los Angeles, as well as the L.A. of 50 years ago. Old-school suspense at its best.

Also from Truth Serum Press

http://truthserumpress.net/catalogue/

Deer Michigan

978-1-925536-25-6 (paperback)
978-1-925536-26-3 (eBook)

"Something quite wonderful happens when you allow yourself to drift through life without a plan of direction," writes Jack C. Buck. *Deer Michigan* takes this heart, embracing the flux of fate in over fifty ethereal narratives. In one story we meet an exiled Mao on a hiking trail, in another the narrator mourns the graceful disappearance of birds. Buck's stories ripple with nostalgia, a reverence for the natural world and an America with room in which to wander. Though the stories in *Deer Michigan* are short, they bottle up an expanse of human experience, offering a stunning universe of feeling.

Also from Truth Serum Press

Hello Berlin!

978-1-925536-11-9 (paperback)
978-1-925536-12-6 (eBook)

Paul is an average Joe from London. He arrives in Berlin during the exciting noughties and discovers a world of free love, free afternoons and lofty literary pursuits. Clueless and curiously innocent, Paul steals the hearts of those around him, leading to anything but a tender love story. Fresh and honest.

www.ingramcontent.com/pod-product-compliance
Lightning Source LLC
Chambersburg PA
CBHW020626250626
47154CB00004B/1685